CATRIONA'S ISLAND

Florence McNeil

August 14, 1990
with love,
Daddy
and mamma.

A Groundwood Book
Douglas & McIntyre
Vancouver/Toronto

For my mother, Jean,
my aunt, Mary,
and my uncle, John,
who came to Canada
from the misty isles.

Groundwood Books/Douglas & McIntyre Ltd.
26 Lennox Street, Third Floor
Toronto, Ontario M6G 1J4

Canadian Cataloguing in Publication Data

McNeil, Florence 1937
Catriona's Island

ISBN 0-88899-076-6

I. Title.

PS8575.N43C37 1988 jC813'.54 C88-094867-1
PZ7.M35Ca 1988

Design by Michael Solomon

Printed in Canada

1

ALL I could think of, all through the graduation ceremonies, was that I'd soon be home. All through the school song, when the choir sang, "We will love you forever, dear Lord Sumner High," and the long speech by some judge who had gone to the school ages ago, and who talked so low you could hardly hear him, except he said something about glorious opportunities for youth even in the midst of a Depression. Even when they got to the prizes and nearer to where they were going to call our names to come up to the stage, all the time I kept saying to myself, "I'm going home, I'm going home" — saying it in time to the beat of the raindrops flowing down the window glass in small translucent drops. It was all I could think of.

I was sitting behind May Douglas and Sheila Brown — the two most popular girls in grade twelve, and they looked ever so smart in white voile dresses with huge flouncy sleeves. I thought I looked pretty good. Mrs. Johnstone, whose house I stayed at in Vancouver, had given me ideas on dressing and fixing myself up, and she loaned me her dress — a pretty one, crepe with a big collar — but it was a little too big for me, even when I tied the sash tight. And the worst of it was that it wasn't exactly white, which we were supposed to wear for graduation — more like ivory, and I was the only one who didn't have white on.

It would be terrible going up on the stage with an ivory dress that was too big — but at least it would soon be over. All over. The long year at the high school in Vancouver.

It wasn't totally bad, of course. I couldn't say that. There was Clara who was a good friend. I was sitting beside her, and I grinned at her, and she brought her shoulders up in an excited shrug. In some ways we looked alike. We were both tall, the tallest girls in our class, big-shouldered — the opposite of May and Sheila, who were what the magazines call "petite."

I'm like my grandfather, strong, big, and at the lighthouse that's a great advantage with all the hard work to do. But not such an advantage in the city, at school.

How I looked had begun to preoccupy me in the city. I'd never thought much about my looks before; but away from my grandparents, away from our island, at school in the city, it was as if I had become someone else and I didn't know who that somebody was.

Then they were calling out the names of the prize winners. I didn't think I'd get a prize. Not that I wasn't pretty good in my subjects, but the one I was best at — art — was not considered too important at the school, and there was no prize.

Mr. Simpson, the art teacher, only came in two half-days a week, and he was very old with a grey walrus moustache that wobbled when he talked. I liked him because he told me constantly that I had real talent. (He never got my name straight; "Cynthia," he called me.) "You should pursue an art career, Cynthia," he always said. "Go to the art school."

Up till then I'd never heard of "art careers." Art was just something you did.

I watched Willie Basheart go up to get his prize in Latin, and I looked at Clara and rolled my eyes, and she started to giggle — little strangled giggles that she tried to cover over with coughs.

We'd drawn lots for partners for the graduation dance the night before, and I'd got Willie, who was as short as I was tall, and couldn't dance. The two of us were out there looking foolish, with Willie hardly coming up to my shoulders and dancing facing out to the side like he wanted to run away.

I wasn't used to that kind of dancing, slow, with a partner, because in Scotland our dances were quick, vigorous — quadrilles, scottisches — jumping around, so that it didn't matter if you weren't exceptionally graceful.

Still, I got through the night, and a couple of boys even asked me to dance, and there was lots of good food, and lemonade, and balloons flying all over at the end of the evening, and girls with tears in their eyes having their pictures taken under the banner that said, "Class of '32."

Then it was time to get our diplomas. My hands started sweating and I wiped them with a hanky from the box Mrs. Johnstone had given to me, pretty linen hankies with tiny embroidered sprigs of heather in the corner.

The principal was calling the names in alphabetical order. "Peter Allandale," he called out. Peter went up, standing very straight. He was a military cadet. "Christine Arthur." Her hair had become blonder and blonder as the year went on, and now seemed to be verging on green. I didn't think I could ever dye my hair. I would just leave it brown —

brown and straight, fastened with a barrette. Curling it just didn't seem to work very well; it went into a frizz.

The students going up to the stage were smiling for the most part, though the smiles looked strained, and you could tell everyone was nervous. I hoped I could get through it all without tripping. The steps to the stage looked steep, and I had on high heels, specially bought for the occasion — strapped white sandals that I'd got for a dollar, out of the two dollars I got from Mrs. Johnstone for helping out. I wasn't used to wearing them.

I turned to look back into the audience, and I could spot my grandmother's navy-blue straw hat, dented and floppy, and my cousin Morag with a big hair ribbon on top of her head, and my Auntie Agnes. My grandmother had stayed with her the night before when she came down on the boat. I smiled at my grandmother and she said very loudly, "Hello there, Catriona," and that sent Clara off into giggles again.

They were at the L's now — James Logan, then Jeannette Marsh and Mary Morrison. And then, "Catriona McLeod." It was my turn. I got up, taking a deep breath, my feet wobbly in my new sandals.

I got to the stage and walked over to Mr. Jensen who reached out to shake my hand. For a moment I could hardly reach out my arm. It was as if I was paralyzed, stiff, as if it didn't belong to me. But somehow I did it and took my diploma in its blue ribbon, and headed down the steps on the other side. I could hear some clapping, mostly coming from where my grandmother was sitting, while Mr. Jensen called out, "Richard Mc-

Millan." And then I was back in my place and it was over.

I was so shaky that my jaw was wobbling. Clara had come back to her place and was leaning towards me, saying, "It's over," and we were both sighing loudly.

I was feeling lightheaded. This year at school had made me wonder if I was coming down with the nerves, like my grandmother has, though my Auntie Jessie says she's strong as an ox. But she gets these nervous attacks with headaches, and she says it's in the family, that my mother had them, too. I scarcely remember my mother. She died when I was four years old and the next year my father was lost at sea. I'd always lived with my grandparents. But maybe it was all too true. Maybe I was going to be a nervous wreck, like my grandmother says she is most of the time.

Then the ceremonies were over. We sang "God Save the King," and Mr. Jensen was inviting everyone to the school cafeteria for tea and sandwiches. People were milling around, and some of the girls were crying.

Clara gave me a big hug. "We did it all right, Catriona." She was fiddling with the blue ribbon on her diploma. "I thought I'd die."

"Me, too," I said. Then Clara's mother came over and my grandmother and the other relatives all seemed to reach us at the same time. So everybody introduced everybody.

"Isn't it nice to see the girls graduating?" Clara's mother was tall, with a pointy face like Clara. "I think an education is so important in these hard times, don't you?" She said that to my grandmother, who was looking at me and smiling. I hadn't seen her smile so much for a long time. She usually looks stern, but she's got a nice smile, even though she has to be careful of her false teeth, which she says the old "mearlach" (which is "thief" in Gaelic) dentist sold her without giving her a right fit.

"Och, it's wonderful," she said. "And her only just turned seventeen and all." She reached out and gave my shoulder a couple of pats.

"Aye, it is and all," my Auntie Agnes said. "She's a clever girl, Catriona."

My grandmother took her crumpled hanky out of her purse and wiped her sweating face. "It's a pity your Allister couldn't have been finishing. But then he never took to the books like our Catriona." She said it triumphantly, and Auntie Agnes looked a little hurt. She fanned her round face with the program.

"We can't all be scholars," she said.

"And he's got a good job," cousin Morag put in. She was working as a maid in a big Vancouver house. "On the wharves, steady work, too..." She nodded her head, and the big hair ribbon bounced on her hair which was sticking out and frizzy. She'd had it permed, she told me. It seemed like a lot of torture, sitting under those huge electric rollers. Morag had showed me where she'd had her scalp singed, and I told her she was daft. She said you had to move with the times.

"Ah, well," Clara's mother said. "It's wonderful to have a steady job."

"There's nothing steady nowadays," my grandmother said. "Even us keepers. They say they're going to turn them all on to the electrification, and who knows who'll be left?"

"Keepers?" Clara's mother looked puzzled.

"Lighthouse keepers," Auntie Agnes said. "Mairi and her husband are on a lighthouse, up the coast a ways. You wouldn't catch me on those places in a hundred years."

"No one asked you," my grandmother muttered.

"Lighthouses," Clara's mother opened her eyes even wider. "How romantic."

"No, they're not," said my grandmother. And just then the principal said again through the microphone that the tea was being set out, and we could see the crowds thinning out in the auditorium, so we all moved away.

The cafeteria was crowded and noisy, and there were grade eleven students serving the graduates and their parents and friends. The tea was very nice, though my grandmother said it was too weak. "Make tea, make tea," she said in Gaelic. "Make water, make water." She always went off into Gaelic, expecially when she was telling you old sayings. I could see people around us looking at her. They were probably thinking we were foreigners. As if the Hebridean Islands in Scotland weren't part of the British Empire.

"I'm that hungry," Auntie Agnes said. She was on her second plate of sandwiches. Little dainty ones, they were, circles and squares, filled with salmon and tuna and egg, all fancy looking.

I didn't feel too hungry, though. And I didn't feel like staying around. I wanted to be away. I wanted to see the island again and the lighthouse and my grandfather. Everyone seemed to be enjoying themselves, but mostly what I felt was an immense sense of relief. I was so glad the school year was over.

Some of the students stopped to say goodbye — and a few of the teachers. My history teacher, and the librarian, who knew me from taking out so many books, and old Mr. Simpson, peering very closely at my grandmother, his small round glasses sliding down his nose, a teacup clattering in his hand.

"Hello, there, Cynthia," he said.

My grandmother stared at him.

"You must be Cynthia's mother." He shook her hand, and nodded at me. "She has real talent, this young girl, real talent." Then he wandered off to another table.

"Who was that?" My grandmother kept staring at Mr. Simpson as he left.

"My art teacher," I said.

"Art." My grandmother waved her hand with a sandwich in the air. "Nonsense, the lot."

"Catriona's real good at art, Mrs. McLeod," Clara said. She was nibbling on two egg sandwiches at once.

"Aye," my grandmother conceded. "She's always making pictures. Always since she was a little girl. Her great-grandfather before her, he was always making pictures. He made this picture of a horse, you'd swear it was alive, and all." My grandmother took a slurp of her tea, and then fanned it with her hand. "Tea's hot, even if it's weak."

"I hear Catriona is going to be a teacher." Clara's mother looked at me. "Are you going to teach art?"

"She'd be better off to teach something useful, like doing sums."

Auntie Agnes tugged at her collar. Beads of sweat stood on her neck. "It's settled then, Catriona. You'll be going to Normal School next year to train to be a teacher."

"Aye," my grandmother said emphatically. "She is."

Then Clara's mother asked my grandmother about the lighthouse, and my grandmother went on and on about how hard a life it was but with an underlying pride in her voice that made you realize she really did like it.

I was just sitting there, half listening. There was all this talk swirling about me, and I wasn't saying anything.

Because I'd made up my mind. I hadn't said anything to anyone yet, but I'd made up my mind. I wasn't going to be a teacher. That had seemed all right in the old country, but not here. I wasn't going to stand up in front of another class, even if I was teaching it, and I wasn't going to spend another year in the city.

I wasn't going back.

— 2 —

IT took four hours to get to Buccaneer Cove from Vancouver. You had to take a boat up the coast because there was no road. I was so anxious to see my grandfather, who would pick us up at the ferry pier and then take us to the island, that the boat seemed to not be moving at all. Just standing still in the middle of the strait. But it was sunny, not like graduation day, and my grandmother and I were sitting on the deck, and even though it was breezy it wasn't cold a bit. It was so nice to just sit. I hadn't realized how tired I was.

"That's a nice school you had there." My grandmother wanted to chatter about everything. She hadn't been in the city in over a year, since we moved to the lighthouse.

"It was all right," I said. I really didn't want to talk, but to sit and look at the islands with their trees coming right down to the water, rounded and furred, like cats. Not like our island in Scotland, which was jagged and almost treeless. In the distance I could see an island with a small mountain that ended in an anvil shape, and I wanted to draw it. Old Mr. Simpson had said real artists see the world in shapes, not colours. I believed that. I know I'm not truly an artist but I'm always noticing shapes of things. Shapes that are there and then change. Sometimes it's odd how I see things. It reminds me of the fun house mirrors at the Vancouver exhibition where everything changes shape —

the walls and pillars, even myself, floating and tearing in half and coming back together.

I see the world like that, and I would like to hold the shapes still long enough to draw them, so when they're gone I'd have them on paper.

The boat was turning out of the sun. My grandmother, who had just draped her sweater over her shoulders, buttoned it up. "Brrr, it's cold now," she said. Then she added, "But there was lots of sun came into that bedroom of yours at the Johnstones. You could tell that was a warm house and all. Not like the lighthouse."

"But I would stay at the lighthouse any day," I said. "Compared to the city."

My grandmother looked at me. The wind had blown the brim of her hat up, and she pulled it down with both her hands. "What are you saying? Freezing to death, with the moss creeping over everything, and the heating going out sometimes and all, no electricity.... It's no life at all, especially for women. Now look at Agnes, there, comfortable, with the electric light and a real oil stove and an electric ice box. And Donald, he only works down at the railroad tracks, so it's not that they've got lots of money. And her telling us about all the work out here — I mind that — all the time." My grandmother made a snorting noise through her nose that ended in "brmpprr."

"I know, Granny," I said. My grandmother always brings that up. That's why we'd come out. Back in Scotland my grandfather had been a ship's carpenter, and away in the boats all the time, and he was tired of it, and my grandmother was tired of having the responsibility of the croft, though I did my fair share — rushing home from school to help feed the chickens or gather nettles to feed the cows, and then leading them home. I loved the cows. I can still see them so clearly — their kind faces and huge horns like trumpets that stuck out of their heads.

When I think of the old country now it always seems to have been summer. At least, that's what I remember mostly. Chrissie my girlfriend and I would help to cut the peats, smelling the fragrant heather smell, standing in the sun looking out at the ocean that surrounded our island on all sides. Then there would be a few scones, a cup of tea for lunch. We were both going to be teachers, Chrissie and me. It seemed right, then. We'd have this cottage where we'd stay together, and we'd buy all the cookies and candies and white bread out of the little store, and eat everything we wanted, and be respected by everyone on the island for being teachers.

It was wonderful to plan, with the sun warming our faces, the whole of summer, its promises, at our feet. I have these pictures still in my mind. Chrissie and me climbing the cliffs to look for birds' eggs, sometimes Morag coming along, but hanging back, scared, while we stood on ledges, jutting over the boiling sea, so far down that gulls looked finger sized. Or taking out the small rowboat, with me rowing, usually, bouncing in the waves, the stormier the better, sneaking out, and worrying my grandmother who was sure we'd be drowned. And I remember times alone, without Chrissie, sitting quiet on a hill among the short grass and the heather and primroses, looking down at the island, following the lines of hillocks and scrub trees and then trying to draw what I saw.

I liked school and my friends at school, and in those days I was always sure of everything. I remember Miss Cameron, our teacher in the infant school, asking us if we knew what we were going to be when we grew up, and me shouting out, "a teacher," right away, and Miss Cameron saying "Well, there's a little girl who knows her own mind." It was all planned.

Then everything changed when Auntie Agnes wrote us about all the work over here in Vancouver, and a lot of Hebrideans were out in Vancouver already. "Come out," she wrote. Even now she tells us there was work. "Aye," she says, "three years ago there was this talk of a bridge across the inlet. There was all these big fancy houses going to be built at the university, and didn't Colin Beag get a job for himself building in a factory, or something. There was lots about..."

It wasn't like that at all.

We didn't have a good start. It was a terrible time to come out, in the middle of a Depression, my grandfather leaving the boats, selling our croft, the whole world changing quickly. And me with only a year to go for my School Leaving Certificate. And I was hugging Chrissie goodbye, both of us crying like we'd never stop. And then I was in the ship and watching the island now green through my tears so it was blurred, its lines fading, washing away.

Then there was the long ship voyage, the creaking train all the way to Vancouver, where it turned out there weren't any jobs at all. Nothing. Worse than the old country. And these poor men everywhere — all over the streets — sleeping on sidewalks, knocking on your door for a cup of coffee, in tatters, their eyes sunken and hopeless.

So we had to move into Auntie Agnes's basement in the east side of Vancouver. It was dark and you could smell mould, and I didn't even have a bedroom, just an alcove with a roll-up bed. I cried myself to sleep in that gloomy basement with all the city noises around, cars that never seemed to stop, and trains and streetcars and such crowds of people out there. I felt choked by them. So many people. I had never seen so many faces together — faces that were strange and unfriendly, staring.

And at night sometimes I could hear my grandmother crying, too, and my grandfather saying, "Isht now. It will be all right." Sometimes just before I went to sleep I would picture what we'd left. The small island, secure, friendly, so familiar I could draw it all from memory.

That terrible time at Auntie Agnes's in the damp basement seemed like months and months — we were that unhappy. Only my grandfather stayed as cheerful as he could, like he always did, going out every day to look for work. Until the lighthouse keeper's job came up and my grandfather got it on the spot, because the old keeper was ill and they needed someone immediately. So he was hired by the marine department and allowed to take along Colin, who'd been on the boats with him, for an assistant.

—3—

We soon found out about the island. Heron Island. Our new island replacing the one we'd left in the old country. An island in the inner passage, only two miles from shore, set out like a long whale, its head rocky and clustered with white buildings that ended in the tall lighthouse tower the back furred with trees that faded off into the ocean. The cottage with real plumbing — a porcelain bathtub and a neat little kitchen that made my grandmother's eyes sparkle when she saw it. A real phone attached to a radio — my grandfather's pride and joy — and upstairs my own bedroom that looked out over the sea to the mainland, giving me new pictures to fill my mind.

I hadn't wanted to leave Heron Island for the city. I thought maybe I could finish my schooling by correspondence. But the department of education said even with the time I'd missed in moving, I had an education equal to grade eleven, and if I wanted to go to Normal School, I'd need a year in a British Columbia school. And so, after only four months, I had to leave my new island to go to the city.

* * *

We were coming closer and closer all the time.

My grandmother and I had lunch on the boat. It was pleasant sitting at the table by the window eating a roast beef dinner, even though I was getting more and more impatient. I knew it wouldn't be long now. It was good to look out at the calm ocean, noticing all the sea things — a tug boat pulling a long raft of logs with seagulls perched on them, a big motorboat, a yacht and people who waved at our boat.

"Look at this," my grandmother said, picking up a corner of the table cloth. "It's real linen and all. Just like Mrs. Johnstone has in her house."

"Mmmmm," I said. I was getting so excited. In the distance I could see the pier, and the waiters were starting to hurry people out of the dining room.

I'd be home soon.

Finally, after what seemed hours, the boat shoved its way into the pier, and I looked for my grandfather in the crowd at the dock — summer cottagers meeting friends, and people waiting for mail and groceries. I grabbed my grandmother's hand and pulled her along. "Come on, let's go," I said, and tried to shove through the crowds on deck. I kept looking over the people at the wharf. All of a sudden I saw my grandfather. He hadn't seen us yet.

"There he is, there he is," I waved. "Grandpa," I yelled. He was looking at the boat, his hand shielding his eyes from the sun.

"Och a Dia, he can't hear you," my grandmother frowned. "Look at him, he's got on his old hat. If I'm not around to see he's dressed proper..."

My grandmother's voice faded out, and I ran ahead, and I was hugging my grandfather and he was saying, "Meudal, meudal," which is "my dear" in Gaelic, and sounds ever so soft and nice.

"Och, and I'm glad to see you..." He stepped back and looked at me. It struck me all of a sudden that there was something different about him. His face seemed to have no colour. "And look at you, you're getting bigger and bonnier all the time. And you're looking fine, too, Mairi." He grinned at my grandmother and she nodded.

"It's nice to see you, Ian. Now take off that old hat. You've got a better one than that." She looked at the dark tweed cap with its grease stains.

"Dia, Mairi, I can't take it off and go bare-headed." My grandfather looked indignant. "I'm saving the other one for good."

"And when is that, anyway?"

My grandfather didn't answer. He was picking up our suitcases and the box tied with rope. "Come on, then, follow me. The yacht's waiting down the dock."

We followed him down the steep wooden steps that led to the small wharf beside the pier where people could leave their boats. It was very hot and the smells of tar and motor gas seemed to rise up like they were boiling together. My grandmother was having a hard time coming down the steep steps, trying to walk between the treads, her feet awkward in laced oxfords with thick heels, higher than she usually wore.

My grandfather's "yacht" was tied to the dock. It was a small wooden clinker-built boat that had drifted in one day to the island and which he said was meant for him. He'd asked Colin, his assistant, to buy him a second-hand inboard engine for it. And Colin dutifully did get one — a used one he bought from an old fisherman. Colin has a little bit of what he calls "me own money" left to him by his mother, and so he's a good help to my grandfather, who knows how to get him to part with it.

We climbed into the *Wanderer*, which was what my grandfather had called the boat because it had just wandered in, and sat on the wooden seats he had built around the sides. He pulled at the wrapped cord of the motor which uncoiled, then cursed it a couple of times, pulled it again and it started. I noticed how the pulling made him out of breath. The *Wanderer* was a cranky boat and he always said half drunk most of the time, and inclined to do what it wanted to.

And then we were away, out on the sea which was almost purple today, deeper and darker than the sky. The cool breeze felt so good. My grandmother, who had never stopped complaining of the heat, said, "Ah, thank God," as the little boat headed out, away from the crowds at the dock with their picnic baskets — the summer people whose cottages lined the shore at Buccaneer Cove where the ferry landed. The cottages became smaller while up above them the trees rose higher and higher. From our boat they looked as if they could swallow the cottages. And it was so quiet. I'd forgotten in all the months in noisy Vancouver what real quiet was. All I could hear was the even strokes of the inboard, the light splashing of waves and the squawking of gulls gathered around a fishboat in the distance, its nets draped into the ocean.

"Oh, Grandpa," I said, "you don't know how wonderful it is to get home. I'm going to take off these stockings first thing." I unbuckled my white sandals and then rolled down the elastic at the tops of my stockings and pulled them off. It felt so good, bare legs, bare feet. I swerved around and dipped my feet into the ocean. The *Wanderer* dipped sideways, too.

"Be careful, Catriona! Don't bounce around in the old girl. She's getting crankier all the time," my grandfather said. My grandmother was sitting up very straight. She'd taken her hat off and the wind was making her grey hair, tied in a bun, stick out in small frizzy pieces. "Do you think we can be talking to this educated girl here? I think she's too good for the likes of us and all..." He winked at me, and my grandmother set off telling him all about the graduation and how good I looked and then all about the city and its shops, which made her think of my grandfather's hat again.

"Och, and I'm that mad at myself. I was meaning to go to the shops and get you the summer straw, so you could leave off wearing that terrible thing." She rolled out the *r*'s in terrible.

My grandfather shook his head. "I wouldn't wear a straw hat if you bought it, Mairi."

"Everyone, all the men, wear them in the city, Ian."

"That may be, but I would feel daft going around like I was in high society. Aren't I already in my going-ashore clothes? A clean shirt and all. Dia, you'd have me dressed up like I was the stuffed shirt, or a corpse in a funeral parlour." He pushed the tiller gently away from him, his eyes watching the sea all the time.

My grandmother looked shocked. "Don't be saying those things." Most of the Hebrideans believe that words could do magic things. Things could come true, you could put curses on people with words. All the Hebrideans like words. My grandfather especially. He says words over and over, words he likes the sound of, words he writes sometimes in his log book which he has to keep at the lighthouse — "calm and cloudy," "calm and hazy," "soft sea swells." I hear him repeating them like a poem. He enjoys keeping the log. He wasn't educated, my grandfather, but he's learned a lot himself, and I think he's one of the cleverest people I know.

I like words, too. I've listened to stories and poems all my life, but how I like to put things down is sketch them. I wanted to put things down exactly as I saw them and felt them.

Like this minute we had turned the corner past a spit of land reaching out into the ocean, and there not far away I could see our island outlined against the dark sea, as if someone had put a pencil line around it. The white tower with its lantern ending in its top of red, the white cottages with red roofs all dazzling, and behind them the forest of gnarled firs and pines, swept back by the wind, so they stood with bare trunks in front, their branches reaching backwards like people stretching their arms out behind them.

"It's so beautiful. I really forgot it was so beautiful." I stared at the island. I almost felt like crying.

"Aye," my grandfather nodded. "It is and all. You haven't seen it now since Christmas. That's a long time, Catriona."

My grandmother was staring, too. "Back to the misery," she said, but I could tell by her eyes she was getting excited. "Slave labour. Dia, Ian, if you'd seen the modern (she pronounced it *moderun*) conveniences Agnes has, and warm all the time."

My grandfather winked at me. He always says my grandmother's bark is worse than her bite. He says it's best to let her have her head, like cranky *Wanderer*. You can't fight with my grandmother or the *Wanderer*, that's what he says.

As soon as he'd tied up the boat on the island at the wharf, with its huge derrick looming over it for the supply boat, my grandfather said, "All right now, tea time for the travelling ladies." And we walked towards the cottage, its white walls and small paned windows gleaming in the sun, and the trellis that my grandfather had built filled with my grandmother's roses and sweet peas.

"Oh, it looks so wonderful," I said. We went inside, though I wanted to run around everywhere and look at everything, it had been such a long time. I wanted to look at the outbuildings where we keep our supplies, at the foghorn building, at the chickens, at my grandmother's garden. Most of all I wanted to climb the tower where, from the top, I could see the ocean become small, and I could peer through the trees and mountains into everything hidden — little lakes and hills and mountains you didn't know were there. The whole world spread out in front of you.

— 4 —

But I was glad enough to be in the little kitchen. My grandfather said we were lucky to have our own cottage, apart from the lighthouse. "Take that outfit up on Paradise Rocks," he'd said. "Over on the west coast of Vancouver Island. A whole family living below the tower, standing one on top of each other in one room. By God, we're always lucky, us McLeods."

"We could have had a kitchen a little larger than this one," my grandmother had said, but she liked it well enough, you could tell. It had a real wood stove and a sink with running water. In the old country we cooked over the open fire in the fireplace, and brought water from a well.

My grandfather wiped off the oilcloth on the kitchen table and stuck some wood in the stove and put on the kettle. He was moving about slowly, I thought. My grandmother took off her sweater and slung it over a chair. "It's really too hot for the stove," she said. "With the oil stove now, like Agnes there, you can cool it down quicker, and turn it on when you want it. And then the electric ice box..."

"We have a lovely cooler here," my grandfather said and opened a door to where a box was built into the wall, with a screen opening outside. He took a bottle of milk out of it. "What more could we be wanting? Dia, in the old country, what did we have? No stove at all, no toilet but the backhouse, and running outside freezing yourself in the rain and all."

"The kettle's boiling." My grandmother was looking around now. She had to check up on my grandfather's housekeeping. But the patterned linoleum was clean as a whistle, and everything neat and tidy. My grandfather's pretty good at that — after his years on the boats where he had to keep everything ship-shape.

"I'll bet you're glad to be here, anyway," I said to my grandmother. "I am. I just love it, I really do." I was staring out through the window with its wooden panes, to the rocks that were green with moss and sloped down to the ocean. Just to the side was my grandmother's garden — long rows lined with seaweed for fertilizer. I could see what looked like rumpled bits of green paper dotted here and there — that would be lettuce — and tall onion shoots, and rows of what looked like strawberries.

"Your garden looks wonderful, Granny." I couldn't wait to get out. My grandfather set out the tea and I sipped it quickly.

My grandmother's face relaxed and the stern lines disappeared. "Aye, it is and all, and I'm growing all these Canadian vegetables — lettuce and strawberries — and there'll be the early potatoes soon..." Her voice got enthusiastic. My grandmother is a great gardener, and in the rocky soil on our old island in the Hebrides she had cabbages and Brussels sprouts and all sorts of things growing. The best garden on the island, everyone said.

My grandmother was sipping her tea and starting to look contented, and my grandfather was saying over and over how good it was to see me again, and he was saying it was a pity it was for such a short time. I was going to tell them right then and there that I wasn't going back. But I didn't. I decided I'd go out and look around, and think of how to say it — putting it off, really, because it was hard to do.

"I'm going to wander around out there a bit," I said. "I want to see everything..."

"Everything is all the same, Catriona," my grandfather laughed. "Just waiting for you to come back. You can take the night watch tonight, if you want to. Colin won't mind."

I grinned at him. On a lighthouse the day watch is easy. It is the night, sunset to sunrise, that's hard — watching for fog, making sure the light stays on, winding it every three hours to keep it revolving.

"Sure, I wouldn't mind. I could do it," I said. "I can start the foghorn and put on the light and everything, so why couldn't I take the watch. Why not?"

"Och, get away with you, you're too educated for that." My grandfather poured my grandmother another cup of tea and I went out and just stood for a minute looking around.

When I left the old country — our other island — I didn't think I'd ever love anywhere like I loved it there. But as I looked at the lighthouse tower, the two little outbuildings, the garden, the rocks that went in a see-saw pattern up and down, the gnarled forest beyond, I realized that I loved this place just as much. People in the city used to ask me if I was lonely on the island, but I never was. There may have been only the four of us, but we were always busy and ships came by constantly — steamers and launches and fishing boats — people dropping by to chat and have a cup of tea. And it was so beautiful.

Right away I felt like putting it down in a drawing — but real well, like real artists do.

I walked along the mossy rocks. It felt good. I was still barefoot. I was used to that. I went barefoot all summer in the old country. My grandfather says the old country gives you feet of leather. It was so quiet. I took in deep breaths of air and ocean, even the pungent smell from low tide with seaweed and barnacles decaying on washed-up logs. Everything smelled wonderful.

There was the tower now in front of me, snow-white, reaching up into the sky — one of the highest lighthouses around. At the top the lantern, a glass face with a bright-red bonnet. I walked by the outbuildings: the generator plant that gave us electricity and the brickhouse that housed the foghorn — the machine that split the air with its wail on foggy days or nights. Then I reached the tower ramp and walked in through the white wooden door, running past the bare concrete floor with the steel tanks of kerosene neatly tucked into the walls.

Looking up, I could see the stairs that spiralled around and around up towards the light. I started running up the iron steps, holding onto the rail, excited at being there again, when I stubbed my toe hard and had to stop for a minute.

I stood on one leg and hugged my foot, saying, "Ouch."

Then, just then, I looked back and down. And it was so strange. I was suddenly afraid. My legs felt like jelly, I got that scared. I kept telling myself it was daft. I'd been up the tower a hundred times. But I was scared now, scared of being up so high. And scared of going down, suspended there, my hand sweating on the railing, waves of fear going through me.

I wouldn't keep going up. That was certain. So, taking a deep breath and saying a little prayer in Gaelic, I held on, turned around, sat down and pulled myself down one step at a time, ever so slowly. It seemed like a thousand steps. It was not only steep, but somehow smothering. The white concrete walls, which had seemed at one time like enchanted castle walls to me, now made me think of stories I'd heard about people buried alive in dungeons. I didn't think I would ever get down. But finally I reached the last step and I ran out, my legs trembling.

And then, once outside, I felt foolish. What was wrong with me? Me, who helped my grandfather at the lights, who'd sat up there and watched him at his log book, enjoying the view, looking through the glass...who'd stood outside against the railing, polishing the glass to make it sparkling clear. What had happened to me?

I sat down on a log, and gradually the trembling stopped. And I thought about this new me. What had happened? Had the city changed me?

I had been proud of the way I'd behaved in going to the city, answering Mrs. Johnstone's ad for a student for home help, making my own way without depending on my relatives. Mrs. Johnstone had turned out to be very kind, but from the beginning I'd felt as if I didn't belong, with my bulky home-knit sweaters and tams, my accent which I was constantly reminded of.

The first week of school I was reciting a poem we'd had to memorize — a poem about autumn — for English class. I said the wrong word, stopped, put my hand over my mouth and said, "Oh, that's daft," and the whole class broke into laughter. I remember feeling my face turning red. Of course, everyone got used to me after a while, but the echo of that laughter stayed with me.

It wasn't that anyone was mean. Mostly they were kind. I was chosen to be on teams for spelling bees, and I always got the hard words, and I even wrote an article for the school newspaper about the island in Scotland, and everyone said nice things about it and asked me all sorts of questions about the old country.

I suppose it was socially that I was left out. I started to envy the smart-looking girls, the ones who dressed in pretty clothes — long slim skirts and silky blouses and sweaters with pompoms and bows — who were always chattering about dates. I never had a date. The boys seemed to like me all right, but no one ever asked me out. I hadn't thought about boys much till then, but suddenly I wanted to be like the popular girls having their pick of boyfriends. I did have some time off. Mrs. Johnstone told me at the outset that when I finished helping with dinner, doing dishes and so on, my time was my own. And so I could go to basketball or football games, or school parties. But always only with Clara. And the boys would grin or say hello but never stay around.

In the city I started to pay attention to fashion. My grandmother had always knitted me sweaters and made me skirts. But now for the first time I wanted to look more up to date.

Mrs. Johnstone gave me tips on dressing and make-up, and she gave me face powder and a dark lipstick that looked funny on me. She also gave me some of her old clothes. The skirts were too small, but the sweaters were fine — very smart, I thought.

I relied on Mrs. Johnstone's advice and pored over her fashion magazines. But try as I might, I didn't look right. I remember once when I set my hair in little kiss curls, the effect was disastrous. The curls looked like corkscrews. Even when I bought a new dainty little crepe blouse for $1.25 out of my pay, I knew I was too big, too sturdy to look good in it. I would never look like May or Sheila.

I think sometimes Mrs. Johnstone knew I was discouraged. "Don't worry if you find things new and strange," she said to me once. "You've made not one but two changes, from Scotland, to a remote island, and now to a big city. You're bound to feel a little confused. It will come."

But it didn't, not really.

Old Mr. Simpson had told us about perspective, about how to make things look close up or far away in our drawings. It was something I had trouble with. My pictures looked a jumble to me. And that's what I think about when I think about the year in Vancouver. It wasn't right. I didn't belong in that picture. I was out of perspective.

And even when I was back on the island it still wasn't right. Something had changed, and I didn't like it.

5

THE next morning when I woke up in my own room, with its whitewashed walls, the bumps painted into it like waves, the first thing I thought about was how happy I was to be home.The second thing I thought about was the tower. It had been in my mind going to sleep, and I kept telling myself over and over not to be foolish. I made up my mind to go right back and climb it, the next day. Because I knew that was the way to do things. If you fail, go right back and try again or you'll be scared forever.

I let the blind up and pulled aside the thick tweed curtain. The tower was right across from me, and it didn't look scary at all. I thought about how many times I'd seen it the way I saw it right then, the white column with mist swirling around the broad white base. Even in late June there were morning mists on the island.

Everything was familiar, safe, wonderful. I never wanted to leave.

And I reminded myself I'd have to tell my grandparents I wasn't going back to the city. I would do it that very day.

I could smell bacon frying in the kitchen. My grandfather was sitting on a stool, taking his porridge out of the pot, and my grandmother in her overall apron was standing over bacon and eggs, holding the ladle in her hand.

"Aha." My grandfather wiped his mouth with his hand. "There she is. And how did you sleep, meudal?"

"Fine," I said. "It's so nice and quiet."

"Too quiet." My grandmother shoved the ladle under an egg.

"Oh, no, it's perfect. It's so noisy in the city." I thought about telling them there and then about not going back. But that didn't seem the moment.

"And what are your plans today? Do you want to help me take some kerosene up to the light?"

I hesitated for a moment. "Sure I do. When?"

"Later. I have to go to the store first."

"All right now," my grandmother said. "Eggs and bacon all ready. You didn't want any porridge first, did you, Catriona? I mind you didn't always like it."

"No, no, I don't want any."

"I suppose," — my grandfather put the porridge pot in the sink and ran water in it — "she's only eating the corn flakes or those cereals full of wind." He winked at me.

"I don't mind porridge sometimes." I brought plates over to the table and automatically took a cloth and washed off the oilcloth covering. I always did that at Johnstones, though Mrs. Johnstone liked a real table cloth starched and neatly pressed.

We sat at the table. "Now we'll say grace." My grandmother blessed herself and said the grace in Gaelic. Then she poured tea for everyone and we started in on the bacon and eggs.

"Now," my grandfather said as he finished his last bit of bacon. "I've got to go over to the wee folk." He looked at me to see if I remembered the joke. I smiled at him. He was talking about the Nomes who minded the general store over on the mainland. The name made my grandfather think of the little people in the old country. There were always tales of wee folk, gnomes, elves, fairy people who lived in the hills. And these Nomes were, in fact, quite small, so the name stuck, at least for my grandfather.

"I've got a list ready, Ian." My grandmother handed him an envelope with a list on the back of it. We picked up groceries once a week from the store. Bigger supplies come on the *Estevan*, the big lighthouse tender.

"Would you be liking a sea voyage this time of the morning, Catriona?" My grandfather was pulling on his sea boots.

"Sure I would," I said quickly.

"Good, go on, the two of you," my grandmother said. "I can get things done easier if I'm by myself. Mind you take a sweater with you. Maybe even your jacket. There's a lot of fog out there this morning."

"Not fog." My grandfather was buttoning up his mackinaw. Then he reached for his old hat hanging on a nail by the door. "Only mist."

"Here, Ian, you take off that hat when you get to the store. I don't know what they'll be thinking of us."

"Och, they can't hardly see over the counter anyway, poor wee folk..." My grandfather laughed to himself, and we left my grandmother rinsing greasy dishes and humming away. That's how I knew that really down deep she was glad to be home. When she hums, she's happy no matter what she says.

The *Wanderer* was crankier than usual, and my grandfather had a terrible time trying to start it, wrapping the rope around the engine and pulling over and over. I could hear him puffing.

"Are you all right?"

His face was white, I thought. Whiter than usual, so that his dark eyebrows speckled with grey hairs seemed to stand out.

"Don't be daft, Catriona. Of course I'm all right."

But I wasn't so sure.

"Are you sure you're fine? You look tired to me." I glanced at him anxiously.

"It's only this damned boat," he said quickly. "I've a good mind to tow her out into the middle of the ocean and set fire to her." Then he stood up, pulled back his shoulders in a stretch and looked her over. "Dia, I'd better not be saying that. She'll be taking it out on me and acting even worse." He spat on his hands, rubbed them and gave the rope a pull again. This time the *Wanderer* started up, and we were away.

"Can I steer?" I asked.

"Of course. Aren't you the best crew I ever had?" My grandfather handed me the tiller, and I set the nose of the boat out towards the distant shore of the mainland. The boat knifed through the water, and small fingers of spray flew up on both sides of the bow.

"I wish the mists would clear," I said.

The mist was rising off the sea, floating in transparent wisps that moved and then disappeared. It gave me a funny feeling, and I remembered the old tales of will-o-the-wisps my grandfather used to tell — strange supernatural apparitions that appeared from time to time, often heralding something terrible that was about to happen.

6

My grandfather was stuffing tobacco into his pipe, packing the curly bits in tight and tamping them down. He looked over to where the sun, still low on the horizon, was appearing through the haze.

"I think it's going to be a warm day. A bit of wind, though. That will keep the heat down. And I don't mind that, too."

The trip to the general store usually took about half an hour. It seemed longer today, but I started to enjoy it more and more. The fresh air, the spray, the transparent ocean with its filaments of seaweed near the surface. My grandfather tied the boat up at the government dock, and we climbed the wooden stairs to the ramp.

By now the mists had cleared, the sun was shining, and a small breeze blew through my hair as we reached the store.

Mrs. Nome was scooping flour out of a bin. A customer stood at the counter — a tall man with a beard that clung to the edges of his chin. I couldn't help staring. I'd hardly ever seen anyone with a beard.

"Hullo, Mr. McLeod. Be right with you. And, Catriona, well, how are you?" Mrs. Nome was putting the bag of flour on the weigh scales.

"Fine."

The man with the beard handed Mrs. Nome a dollar bill, and nodded to us while he waited for change. He looked half asleep. His eyes were red-rimmed like a rabbit's.

"And what are you going to do with the flour? Bake some bread?" Mrs. Nome took off her glasses, blew on them and put them back on. She was very inquisitive. She knew everything that was happening in Cedar Cove.

The man laughed. His whole face changed when he laughed. His eyes crinkled up and the sleepy expression was gone. "Not me. My only accomplishment is pancakes, half the time burnt." He picked up his package and nodded to my grandfather who nodded back to him. "So long, Doris," he said, and went off.

Mrs. Nome frowned. My grandmother said she didn't like anyone calling her by her first name, because she'd heard Mrs. Nome tell someone not to call her Doris. "And she said it real cranky, too," my grandmother had complained. "As if she were society and all, and in a wee place like Cedar Cove. It's not as if she were in Vancouver."

"Wee places are the worst. You know that from the old country," my grandfather had said. "There's always someone thinks they're better than someone else. Me, I treat them all the same."

Mrs. Nome rubbed her floury hands on her apron and then patted her hair, which was set in stiff waves. There were little streaks of flour in the ridges.

"Well, well, how nice it is to see you, Catriona. And now you've graduated and everything. Isn't that wonderful. What are you going to do now? Oh, I remember. You're going to the Normal School. You're going to be a teacher. I think that's just marvellous. Especially for people like you who have just come out and all, getting ahead that way, because of course, immigrants are disadvantaged, Don't I know myself, having come over from England. But, of course, it does help that I came from an English-speaking country." Mrs. Nome's mouth turned up in a smug smile.

"But Scotland is English-speaking, too." I said slowly.

"Oh, of course. I just meant you people speak — what is it — Gaelic, isn't it? That's sometimes hard to overcome, speaking a foreign language. My sympathies are with you, don't misunderstand me."

"It's *not* a foreign language."

"She's done just wonderful," my grandfather said hurriedly. "We're proud of her. Och, she's always been clever, head in a book all her life."

Mrs. Nome tidied up the ball of string that lay looped on the counter. "You know, Depression or no Depression, there's always going to be a need for teachers. Mind you, I don't know if you can get married and keep teaching — taking a man's job. But Catriona's probably in no hurry, are you?" When she smiled wide, I could see she had two teeth missing at the back.

"No, I'm not." I must have sounded snappy because Mrs. Nome looked annoyed.

"Excuse me," she said. My grandfather quickly handed her the list of groceries. "All right, I'll get right onto this. How is your wife, Mr. McLeod?"

"Just fine. Up to her usual form. Pretty good for an old girl, mind you, Doris." Mrs. Nome winced. I knew my grandfather had done that deliberately. "If she slows down I might be trading her in. So if you see any good candidates around, let me know." He said this seriously, and Mrs. Nome looked bewildered.

"Ah," she said, and reached on the shelf behind her for some tins of corned beef.

My grandfather stuck his pipe in his mouth and sucked on it. "Who's the fellow was in here? The one with the goat beard? I saw him on the island a couple of times, down on the lee side. Looked like he was painting — but I never talked to him. Only waved."

"You know, Mr. McLeod," — Mrs. Nome leaned forward confidentially — "he's a doctor. Or was a doctor. He and his wife have this summer cottage — the bright-yellow one two doors from our store — and they've been coming up for a few years now. From Vancouver. I don't know the whole story, but I don't think his wife is with him now."

"Well, good for him." My grandfather winked at me.

Mrs. Nome looked shocked. "It's because he — " She leaned over closer to us and whispered, " — *drinks*."

"Does he, now?" My grandfather didn't look too interested.

Mrs. Nome stood up straight. "And so I think he's had to quit doctoring — just a young fellow, too — and I don't know what he's doing, just wandering around. Fancies he's an artist." She sniffed.

"Och, well." My grandfather lit up his pipe, ignoring Mrs. Nome's frown. "Painting pictures sounds better to me than cutting people open. Catriona, here, she draws good pictures."

I smiled. But Mrs. Nome ignored me. I think she was disappointed at my grandfather's reaction to her news. She busied herself with our grocery order, muttering that she wished Mr. Nome would get back from Vancouver because she could hardly manage the store by herself. But it didn't seem to take her too long to fill our order, and there was no one else in the store or the post office, which was inside a wire cage sectioned off from the big room.

The wind had really come up when my grandfather and I started back to the island. The small ripples had become frothy whitecaps, and the sea was dark and choppy. I turned and looked back at the store etched in white against a darkening sky. Two doors down, a bright-yellow cottage stood out from a background of trees.

"That must be the doctor's cottage there," I pointed. My grandfather nodded.

The sky seemed to be getting blacker by the minute.

"Looks like a storm," I said.

"You've been too long in the city, Catriona. It's only a breeze." My grandfather didn't look at all concerned. And I realized I shouldn't be, either. As if I hadn't been out in the boat in all kinds of weather.

"Do you want to take the tiller again, matey?" My grandfather was pulling at the *Wanderer*'s motor. After two tries, it started. "By God, she's maybe having a change of heart."

"Sure, I'll steer," I said and settled myself down in the stern.

The boat made its way through the inky seas that rose and ended in foam, so that it seemed to lunge at the sea, rising up and then falling with a faint splash of water on the bow. And yet I didn't feel scared. As we headed out farther and farther, the seas seemed to be calmer, which was curious, because usually it's worse out in the open water. I was feeling proud of myself for handling the boat so well.

And then it happened. I can't explain it at all, because the sea now was relatively calm. I'd been talking to my grandfather, looking away for a moment, when I looked up and noticed we were nearing the island, and what I noticed just at that moment was the lighthouse tower looking large, out of proportion, it seemed. A trick of sunlight had left most of the island in darkness. Only the tower was in dazzling sunlight, making it stand out as if it were gigantic.

I gasped. And suddenly I became aware of being out on the sea, on water, in what seemed to me then only a frail shell of a boat. My hands started to sweat.

"Can you take the tiller now, Grandpa?" I asked.

"You're doing fine." He was looking at the island, his cap pushed back on his head.

"Please," I shouted, "please. I don't feel well."

"Meudal," he said with concern, and I scrambled over to let him at the tiller, and sat there, shaking. "What's wrong?"

"I don't know," I shook my head. "Just sort of sick..."

"Och, well, don't you be worrying," my grandfather said soothingly. "You've been in the city too long. And those waves we had — a touch of the seasickness, probably. You just rest, meudal."

"All right," I said. "That's probably what it is." And I took a deep breath and tried to calm down.

But I knew positively it wasn't seasickness.

7

I WAS beginning to worry about myself. Things that had never bothered me before, ever — the tower, the ocean — were becoming frightening. What kind of a person was I turning into? Maybe I *was* inheriting the family nerves, like the story my grandmother had told me about my great-grandmother who had the nerves so bad, she couldn't go out of the house, but sat there in a wooden chair, shaking all day. Maybe I was going to be like that. Maybe it was all the uncertainty. If I wasn't going to teach, what would I do? The old judge at graduation had talked about all the opportunities out there, but I couldn't see them.

But if I had inherited the nerves, I had also inherited the McLeod stubbornness. I wasn't going to give in. So after we got back from the trip to the store and I had some tea, I decided to look in at the tower again. I was going to beat it. I had to.

Colin was on his way into the blockhouse where the foghorn is kept.

"Hullo, there, Catriona. It looks like a bonny day." He was dressed in a heavy patterned sweater and tweed cap, looking more like winter than summer. But he almost always dressed that way.

"It is…"

Colin paused for a minute, took his cap off and scratched his hair. I could tell he had something he wanted to say to me.

"Catriona..." He paused again, then took a soggy-looking cigarette out of his pocket and stuck it into his mouth. "I've been wanting to mention this. Have you seen your grandfather lately? I mean, have you noticed he's slowing up a wee bit?" He scraped a match over his pant legs and lit up the cigarette. Then he looked at me.

"I thought he looked tired, and he gets winded easily when he's trying to start the *Wanderer*'s engine."

"That damn boat. It'll be the death of him. I tell you the God's truth, Catriona. That boat has the curse on it. I think there's someone put the evil eye on it." He looked at me seriously. People from the old country sometimes believe things like that.

I laughed. "Oh, I don't think so, Colin. I think the engine's just not very good."

"It's more than that." Colin shook his head.

"What do you think? You've been around him more lately. Do you think he's really not well?"

Colin frowned, took a drag of his cigarette and said, "I do and all, Catriona. He's getting tired more easy and I know he has the stomach pains sometimes. I mind the way he goes up the tower stairs — slower than ever. And you know on the night watch you're up there all the time." I nodded. "I've been trying to take the night watch more often myself, but he's a stubborn old man, the old bodach, and he says he's all right. But that's a long climb. Maybe, Catriona, you could be running up there sometimes when the light needs polishing, or help take up the kerosene and all that. You being thirty years younger than me and all."

I nodded. Just thinking about it made my legs feel weak.

“I don’t want to worry you, Catriona. I haven’t said a thing to Mairi, though she must be noticing it. I’m not saying it’s anything much, maybe just tired. He’s not as young as he used to be.”

“He should see a doctor.” I felt really worried.

Colin laughed. “As if he would. I said that to him one day, not like I thought there was anything wrong with him, but I said just go and get one of them to look you over. That was one day when he had to sit down after just chopping a few sticks of wood.”

“And of course he wouldn’t go.”

“Och, all he said was he was never going near those quacks because when you went to see them, you ended up dead.” Colin shrugged. “That was all I could do. Maybe you could talk to him, Catriona.”

“Well, I’ll try. Thanks, Colin, for mentioning it.” Colin said he’d better go. He had to take a look at the foghorn — something about the compressor. As he left he touched the rim of his cap. I knew he only did that for ladies. And it struck me that now he thought I was a lady, not a kid anymore.

It was a strange thought.

8

I SAID a quick little prayer in Gaelic that there wouldn't be much wrong with my grandfather. Maybe it wasn't anything but tired, like Colin said. It was hard being a lighthouse keeper — the twelve-hour watches when my grandfather sat with his feet in the open door of the oven and tried to stay awake, the foggy nights when he sometimes had to sit in the blockhouse all night to make sure the horn kept going, the long climb to the tower, the detailed day-to-day record of weather, of ships passing. This part of the coast was relatively peaceful, that was one thing, surrounded by islands, sheltered by Vancouver Island in the distance.

It wasn't like the life of the keepers on the open ocean, on their bleak rocks, facing hurricane winds and waves that splashed onto the base of the lighthouse.

But it was hard enough. And there was many a time my grandfather was out on the seas, hauling in boats, helping people in distress. Even the short time I was on the island I'd gone with him twice to stranded boats, bringing cold, scared people back to the warm kitchen where my grandmother made them hot tea. It wasn't an easy life.

I thought of the bearded man in the store, the one-time doctor, and wondered if he'd see my grandfather. But I decided someone who drinks wouldn't be too trustworthy. I would have to see what I could do.

And I thought as I stood there looking up at the tower, I'd have to pull my weight. My grandfather shouldn't have go up there so often.

I climbed the wooden steps, crossed the ramp and opened the door into the tower. I paused for a moment looking up the circular concrete walls, and then quickly ran towards the steps and climbed up half a dozen or so, holding onto the iron rail. And then it hit me again, a wave of fear so intense that it almost nauseated me. I couldn't go on. And I wasn't even up high. I backed down, my legs like jelly, my palms gripping the rail.

I felt too weak to run, but I wanted to run — far away from the tower, to someplace where I couldn't even see it.

I told myself to stop being foolish. I told myself I'd have to do something. I walked to the pier, to where our small rowboat lay with her painter tied to a cleat. Quickly I untied the rope, pushed the boat out into the water, and jumped in. I wasn't really going anywhere, just proving to myself that I wasn't afraid of something, of the sea where I had felt at home, where I had spent hours swimming, rowing — now calm and so clear it seemed like a fall day rather than early summer.

I peered over the side. A school of tiny fish raced by, so small they were like raindrops, weaving in and out of the bulbous heads of seaweed. I rowed, quietly, gently, by the shore, pleased that I was able at least to do that, but realizing also that I didn't want to go out where it was deep. I only felt at home in safe shallow water.

That afternoon, only Colin went up to clean the light.

—9—

THE next day my grandmother got a call from Auntie Agnes. "Did you hear that?" she said to me when she hung up. "They're coming to visit. She and Morag."

"Are they? I thought Morag was working at that house..."

My grandmother shook her head. "Not anymore. She quit. Can you picture that, quitting a job when they're so hard to find and all. Still, she's not educated like you, Catriona, so there's not much choice. I thank God every day that you're going to be a teacher. Och, your mother and father, God rest their souls, would be so happy."

I wished she hadn't put it that way. I'd have to tell her soon.

"All right, now, if they're coming, we'll have to get busy. Oh, Dia, this poor place." My grandmother looked around and shook her head. "After the place that Agnes has got there. Why are they coming now, I'd like to know. They never visited before."

Still, she looked rather pleased that they were coming. She wondered where to put them.

"How about at Colin's house?" I asked. Colin had his own place, an outbuilding that had been converted into a bedroom and kitchenette.

My grandmother looked at me, astounded. "Are you asking me to put them in that place — the place of an old bachelor where he never washes his socks and has mould growing in his tea pot? Are you daft, Catriona? No, they'll have to go in my sewing room, with the fold-down bed, although Agnes is going to take up all the room in that bed, her being the size she is."

We went into a flurry of cleaning. The linoleum in the kitchen was washed and waxed, the stove-top blacked, the oil lamps polished, the wooden floor of the sewing room covered with a rug that came out of my bedroom.

Colin was sent to meet Auntie Agnes and Morag at the ferry. It was a calm day, but Auntie Agnes, when she arrived, was complaining of how hard it was to sit in a small boat out on the open sea.

My grandmother was standing at the door waiting for them. She had put on her good navy-blue dress, and had taken her apron off.

"Well, well, Agnes," she said. "Come in and have a drop of tea. Here, Colin, take the suitcases upstairs."

"I think I could use something stronger than tea." Auntie Agnes's face was red, and beads of sweat were dripping from her forehead and spreading in two big patches under her armpits.

"I'll make you my special tea, then," my grandfather said. He went to the flour bin where he stored his liquor, and a bottle of brandy appeared in a cloud of white flour. "I always keep a drop," he said, "for my indigestion. This'll cure you of anything."

Auntie Agnes and Morag were both looking around at the kitchen.

"Here now," my grandmother said, "let's go into the parlour where there's more room."

Everyone followed her into the little room off the kitchen, and Auntie Agnes and Morag sat on the mohair couch with its faded turkish pattern across from the little heater set in the middle of the floor. All the furniture had already been at the lighthouse when we came, but my grandmother had added some touches — a few glass vases; a Staffordshire china dog that used to sit on the mantle in the old country, but now sat on the floor; some framed pictures of my mother and father on their wedding day, and of my grandmother and grandfather in a fuzzy snapshot sitting outside our cottage in the old country, with me on my grandfather's lap. Also — and I was hoping Auntie Agnes and Morag would notice — there were two sketches that I'd made. My grandfather had framed them.

We sat chatting while my grandmother brought in the tea, poured it and watched carefully to see that my grandfather wouldn't put too much brandy in. I said I didn't want any, but Morag said she didn't mind a drop or two.

I looked at Morag. There was something different about her, and then I realized. Her hair was blonde, not light brown like it used to be. And her eyebrows were plucked in two very thin lines, which gave her a surprised expression.

"Well, what do you think of our poor place here?" My grandmother sipped noisily at her tea cup. "Of course, it's nothing like so grand as your place..."

Auntie Agnes was looking more relaxed now. "Well, you don't have the room, Mairi, but still and all, it's a home, isn't it? A person's lucky nowadays in these hard times to have a roof over their head."

My grandmother looked disappointed. "We've got the view here. Big people in town, they would pay a lot of money to have the view we have."

"That's true," Auntie Agnes nodded. "Does it get terrible damp here in the winter?"

"In the winter," my grandfather said seriously, "there's this green moss. It climbs up your legs, and you can't wash it off at all. It stays till the sun comes out in the next spring."

"Och, listen to you," Auntie Agnes laughed.

"I'll take you on a tour of the estate when you've finished." My grandfather was pouring a little more brandy in her tea, ignoring my grandmother's frown. "You'll be interested in climbing up the tower now, won't you? There's the finest view in the world from up there."

Auntie Agnes looked down at her fat legs. "Not me. I never saw anything looked so high. I wonder you can climb it yourself."

"I run up there," my grandfather said, "sometimes ten times a day."

Colin and I exchanged concerned looks.

Morag was looking out the window. "I wouldn't mind getting outside. I'm working on getting a tan."

"In my day," my grandmother said, "girls wanted to stay pale. You always covered up in the sun."

"Och, it's all different for the young ones now, Mairi." Auntie Agnes sighed deeply and asked for a refill of tea. She glanced pointedly at the bottle of brandy.

"I'll take you around," I said to Morag. We went outside. The sun was warm and pleasant. I was wearing a thick pink pullover that Mrs. Johnstone had given to me, and it was really too heavy. Morag was wearing a pretty dress with poppies on it. A light breeze blew the filmy collar up around her hair.

"What do you think of my new hair?"

"Nice, Morag. Different."

She nodded. "I lightened it. It's the thing to do. It's called a Jean Harlow hairstyle. You've seen her, haven't you?"

I shook my head. "No, does she live in Vancouver?"

Morag giggled. "She's a movie star, Catriona. Don't you go to the movies? You must have when you lived in Vancouver."

"Once or twice."

"Of course, being up here, you're out of things anyway, aren't you? How can you stand it by yourself here? It gives me the creeps being away from everything like this. What is that?" Morag was pointing to the wind gauge, a triangle with little cups on the ends sitting on a pole.

"That shows you how strong the wind is blowing. See the dial in the centre?"

"Why do you have to know how strong the wind is?" She didn't sound too interested.

"We phone in twice a day to the weather office."

"Oh, whew." Her eyes were fixed on the tower. "That's high. Do you go up there?"

"Yes," I said quickly. "All the time."

"You wouldn't catch me." We were walking along between Colin's house and the foghorn building. Colin had made a path of white pebbles, and Morag was having a hard time walking on them in her white sandals.

"Ooh, I think I've run my stockings," she said, looking down to where a thin ladder had appeared on her instep. "My good pair, too — real rayon."

"Why don't you take them off? I never wear stockings around here. Not good ones. Little socks are all you need, or bare feet."

"Don't feel like getting stuff out of the suitcase yet." She spit on her finger and placed it at the end of the run.

I showed Morag the brickhouse and the supply building and then we looked in at the tower.

She craned her neck upwards to where the stairs circled in their dizzying spiral. "You've got more nerve than me, to go up a place like that. But then, I've always been afraid of heights."

"I remember in the old country," I said, "when you wouldn't go down that cliff with me and Chrissie where we saw the birds' nests. Do you remember that?"

"Oh, that place. I don't remember very much from that place. When I think of how out of date we were. Let's get out of here. It's spooky." She headed towards the door.

"It is not," I laughed. "But let's go if you want to."

The truth was that I couldn't wait to get out of the tower, either.

— 10 —

WE sat on the beach on a log. Morag peeled off her stockings and tucked her toes into the sand. "Mmmm, that feels good. You know, ever since I was working at the Martins', I've had sore feet. I never sat down, never..."

"I heard you quit."

"I did. I couldn't stand it. I'm looking for work now. My friend, Sue, she works at the sugar refinery and she thinks she can get me on there. I don't care, though, not really. I don't intend to work too long. You know what, Catriona? I got a steady boyfriend."

"Do you?" I looked at her, surprised.

She nodded. "It's serious — I'm telling you — we're probably going to get married next year when I'm eighteen. What do you think of that?" She looked at me. Her eyes were full of excitement.

"Really? But you're so young. You're just a few months older than me."

She looked at her nails. They were painted a deep pink. "I'm ten years older than you, really, Catriona. See, I've gone out a lot and had a good time while you've had your nose in the books. I've always looked old for my age, anyway."

I didn't want to tell her that I thought she looked very young. In spite of the blonde hair and thin eyebrows, she had a kewpie doll face, and was plump like her mother, though with Morag the plumpness showed only in her face.

"Now, look, don't you say a thing, Catriona. Not a thing."

"Your mother doesn't know?"

"She knows I got a steady boyfriend, of course. But I was away from home a couple of years, so she doesn't know how steady. She likes him. His name is Jimmy, and he's got a good job. He's a mail clerk, and he's got all kinds of ambition. He's even got a car, a real swell roadster, too. And he says he doesn't care if I'm foreign. He calls me Margo — "

"*Margo*? What's wrong with Morag?" I looked at Morag again. The sun on her hair made it look stiff like bleached grass in late summer. Her complexion in this glare was perfect.

She pulled her dress up above her knees so that the full warmth of the sun fell on her legs. "Morag sounds so — oh, you know — like you just got off the boat."

"That's real daft, real stupid. We're not foreigners." I probably spoke more sharply than I meant to.

"Well, don't bite my head off. You know what I mean — the accent and all, and my mother and father jabbering away in Gaelic. Though lately I've told them to tone it down a bit. But when they get excited, they're at it again."

"Why shouldn't they talk in Gaelic if they want to? He should like you the way you are."

"We've talked about this before, Catriona. You know what I think about it. You've got to fit in over here and the best way to do it is to get rid of the out-of-date things we used to do. Then you'll find a good Canadian fellow like I did — with ambition. Listen, aren't you going to congratulate me on my news?"

"Oh, sure, Morag, of course. If you're happy about it, I think that's great."

"I think so, too." Morag launched into a description of her boyfriend and his plans. I listened in silence, staring out at the water. Far out on the horizon, a sailboat went by, under power, its masts bare. You could hear the drone of the motor.

"I bet you can't wait to get to the city this fall. This may be okay for the summer, the beach and all — but I can't imagine a whole year."

"I like it here," I said. "I don't like the city. I'm not going back."

Morag stared at me. "You're not going back? I thought you were going to be a teacher."

"I don't want to be a teacher now." I made swirly patterns in the sand with my index finger.

"Well! Mind you, I don't blame you. I can't imagine anything worse. But, what will you do? There's no jobs, you know."

"I know. I might just stay here for a while."

Morag frowned. "Here, in this deserted place? When you could be in the city? I don't understand you at all."

I didn't answer. Morag *didn't* understand me. We were sitting so close we were touching, but we had nothing in common. Beside Morag I felt old-fashioned, out of date. Morag was round and delicate, her figure womanly. She was all grown up, engaged. And I had never even had a date.

I didn't seem to be growing up at all.

"What do your grandparents think about all this?" Morag's question startled me.

"They don't know. I haven't got around to telling them."

"They'll have a fit. Your grandmother, anyway."

"Probably. But it's my decision." I sounded braver than I felt.

We both sat for a few moments without saying very much. Then Morag said she'd better unpack her things before they got too wrinkled, and we went back to the house.

My aunt and my cousin only stayed for three days. Mostly Morag and I lay around in the sun. She didn't want to swim because she said the water was too cold. But I went in for a few dips. I'm used to cold water, and I believe what the old people in Scotland believed — that there's healing in the ocean waters.

— 11 —

THE morning after my aunt and cousin left, after my chores, I decided what I wanted to do most was sit and stare at the ocean, without talking or listening. I made myself comfortable on a log and sighed with relief. I was grateful for the quiet after what had seemed like constant chatter. Suddenly, my grandfather was beside me.

"You're looking down in the mouth, Catriona. Are you not feeling well?"

"Oh, I'm all right, really. Tired, maybe."

My grandfather sat down on the log beside me. "Och, well, those two, they're enough to tire out anyone. You know, Catriona, I think I'm getting like the hermits. The fewer people I see, the better — for more than an hour, anyway." He reached into his pocket and stuck his pipe in his mouth, sucking on it without lighting it.

"Maybe I'm like that, too." I smiled at him.

"That Morag, now, she's looking very up to date. I think she's painted her hair."

"She has. Dyed it, that's what it's called."

My grandfather shook his head. "Well, I'm that glad you're satisfied with your own. Och, there's no comparison — the two of you, and she was a nice wee girl and all. Still, just because you stick your head into the paint pot doesn't make you bad, either..." He smoothed the thinning strands on top of his head. "If I could find some more grey hairs to paste on top I'd be doing it, too..." He turned and looked at me. "Here, I'm going up the tower. Do you want to come up and help me check the kerosene?"

I thought quickly. "I've got sore legs. I don't know what I did to them." I thought the excuse sounded thin.

"Maybe it's the rheumatism. Maybe it's damp for you here, meudal. It is for some people, you know. Your grandmother, she gets these aches and pains in the winter. But then," he laughed, "she has so many complaints, I don't know..."

"I don't think it's rheumatism. Maybe I'm not used to so much activity all at once."

"Well, all the same, it's a good thing you're going back to the city, and all. You may be the type is affected by the damp. Not that I won't miss you a lot, meudal."

"I don't know about the city. I'm not keen on going back." I was leading up to it. I don't know why it was so hard to do.

"Aye, I know what you mean," my grandfather mumbled.

I changed the subject. "Are you all right? That's what I'm worried about. It's not too much for you, all the climbing and the watches and all?"

"Me? I'm on top of the world. Never felt better."

"Still," I said carefully, "you know, everyone should have a medical checkup, especially when you're a bit older."

My grandfather took the pipe out of his mouth and shook his head emphatically. "What are you saying? Colin was after me the same way. And your grandmother. And don't I mind in the old country, anyone who went to the doctor, he came home dead."

"Oh, you're impossible," I said. But I couldn't stop worrying. Having visitors was obviously hard on him. He looked whiter than usual — a whiteness touched with grey, so that he seemed somehow very fragile.

I felt terrible that I wasn't helping out, wasn't pulling my weight. Since I got back I seemed to be mostly helping my grandmother — feeding chickens, gathering eggs, cooking meals. I seemed to have changed from my grandfather's helper to my grandmother's. Spending more time indoors than out.

It was the lighthouse work I had liked before. All the spit and polish involved in keeping the great plate glass panels of the lantern at the top of the tower sparkling clean, so the revolving light shone out brilliantly over the sea. That was my favourite job. Lighthouses were like ships. You were always cleaning, always working.

I thought of the other chores I'd done, carrying the gallon drum of kerosene up from the tanks at the base of the tower, pouring it into the small tank beside the light, winding the counterweights that hung down like the weights on a grandfather clock — weights that made the great light turn round and round. I'd loved all the work in the lighthouse. And I'd liked meeting the lighthouse tender, the *Estevan*, when it called once a week with mail and supplies — its decks covered with anchors and chains and buoys.

In the past, I was a lighthouse *helper*. Not like now, when I seemed to be a housemaid.

12

WHEN I went back to the house, someone was going up to the door. It was the man I'd seen in the store — the doctor.

"Oh, hello," he said. "You live here, do you?"

"Yes," I said. "Did you want to talk to my grandfather? He's just out somewhere. My grandmother's in."

"I don't want to bother anyone. I've been around the island a few times doing some sketching and painting. And I'd like to work at this end by the buildings. That's a marvellous lighthouse there. But I wanted to introduce myself. I didn't want to just trespass."

He seemed very polite. But he was dressed like my grandfather in old clothes — a thin sweater with holes in the sleeves, and dungarees. He was hanging onto a straw hat with a torn brim. He smelled faintly of whisky.

My grandmother opened the door. She stopped when she saw the man and stared at him.

"It's all right, Granny. He only wants to paint."

"Does he?" She was still staring disapprovingly, holding the screen door open.

"My name is Harrison — William Harrison — Bill. I live over across the way — Cedar Cove. And you're..."

"McLeod," I said. "I'm Catriona, and this is my grandmother, Mrs. Mairi McLeod."

"How do you do? McLeod — Highland Scottish — am I right? That would account for that delightful accent."

The man smiled. His smile was pleasant, the way I remembered it in the store. His eyes closed almost completely, wrinkles spreading out into his hairline. But in spite of the wrinkles, I could see he was quite young, blue-eyed, deeply tanned, the tan running into the scraggly whiskers that jutted out unevenly around his face.

"From the Hebrides." My grandmother's face had softened. "Would you be wanting a cup of tea, Mr. Harrison? I'll put the kettle on."

"No, no, thank you. I just wanted to let you know I'll be around, so you don't think you're being invaded. Well, I'll set my stuff out. Thanks. Goodbye, Mrs. McLeod, Catriona."

He shoved the torn straw hat on his head and walked away. My grandmother was staring after him.

"Dia, he dresses like a scarecrow. Like your grandfather. I don't know. These artists, you hear about them. Never have any money, just going around like the hobos."

"He's a doctor." I looked out to where Bill Harrison was settling himself on a rock in front of the tower, staring up at it.

"Och, now I know. Mrs. Nome at the store, she was telling me. He's a drinker, that's what she was saying. A clever doctor, and young and all, and he gave it all up for the drink. And he's going around like that. The city is full of the likes of that — sleeping on park benches and all. Businessmen who lost their money in the Depression. I mean, them that hasn't jumped to their deaths from office windows and all."

"Oh, I think a lot of that is talk," I said. "And you know how Mrs. Nome is."

"I know." My grandmother walked back into the house and I followed her. "But look at the look of him. You can tell he's not caring much about anything, poor soul."

My grandmother glanced at the wall clock. "Dia, the time! I'd better be starting in on the stew for your grandfather and Colin. And I'm that tired after having Agnes and Morag. It's all right for them in their house with all the conveniences, not slaving away night and day." She took some meat out of the cooler.

"Well, don't make stew," I said. "It's going to be hot, anyway. How about a salad from the garden?"

"A salad for working men?" Granny snorted. "That might be all right for your Mr. Johnstone in the city, sitting around all day. Here, you peel some potatoes."

I pulled some potatoes out of the bag under the sink and took them to the table. There wasn't room for both of us at the sink. My grandmother was chopping onions vigorously.

"Granny," I said, "I wonder if Grandpa should go to a doctor for a checkup. I think he's failed a bit, don't you?"

She wiped her eyes streaming from the onions. "You know, Catriona, I think so myself. He's slowing up, I can tell that, and he complains of his stomach off and on. Puffing, too, he is sometimes, like a steam train. I said to him, Ian, you maybe got something wrong with you. There was heart trouble in the family, Catriona. His own father, didn't he die of it?"

"Then he should see someone."

"And can you get an old mule to go up hill?" My grandmother snorted. "He won't go near doctors. I've been after him and after him, till I'm afraid to say anything more, he gets that annoyed. And it's hard here, Catriona. Even with Colin, this is hard work for an old man. But, then, how can a person live? There's no jobs anywhere. Sometimes, I think we should have stayed in the old country. If Agnes hadn't sent us out that pack of lies. Och, well, isn't it God's will and all?" She sighed and placed the onions in a neat pile on the cutting board. She started cutting up the meat into small strips, turning the strips over and over in flour.

"Grandpa loves the island. It's just that he should see a doctor and get some pills or something. But I know how he is..." I stared out the window. I could see Bill Harrison, his sketch book opened on his lap, his hand holding a pencil that moved quickly over the paper. "Maybe that doctor..."

Granny looked up. "Who? Oh, him. I'm not asking the likes of him. He'd probably kill your grandfather."

I kept glancing out the window. Watching Bill Harrison made me think about my own art work. I walked into the parlour and surveyed the sketches on the wall. My grandfather had framed them in ornate old frames someone had given him. The frames were too heavy for the simple lines of the drawings. They were of the lighthouse tower as you would see it from the ocean, taken from two different angles, and of the *Wanderer* up on my grandfather's ways, a timbered framework on the shoreline where he works on the boats, with the storage shed behind. My grandfather had thought they were wonderful.

"It's just like you're looking at them. Just like you took a picture."

But as I looked at them, I thought to myself they weren't really very good. They were done before I knew much about drawing, really just out of my head. I could do better now that I'd been at school. I'd brought a book of my school sketches with me, and I ran up to my room and took them out of the bureau drawer. I flipped through the book. They were still lifes — fruit bowls, a vase; an outdoor sketch, a maple tree in the school yard, a house across the street from the school, and one I'd nearly forgotten about — the island from memory, the lighthouse, the outbuildings, the trees stretching back into the sea. I hadn't shown that one to Mr. Simpson. It hadn't been one of our assignments.

I had a sudden desire to take my pictures to show Bill Harrison. I wondered what he'd think of them.

My grandmother was yelling for me. "Catriona, will you go get your grandfather for his tea. I see him over by the blockhouse."

"All right," I said.

My grandfather was pretending to be folding a tarp, but really he was staring at Bill Harrison in the distance.

"Tea time," I said.

"Oh, good." My grandfather kept staring. "Here, Catriona, that's the man we saw in the store. The doctor —"

"Sssh," I said. Bill Harrison had noticed us and was waving. "You better go for your tea. Granny's got it made."

"Aye, I better. Catriona, I'm off to the store again today. Do you want to come?"

"No," I said quickly. "I told Granny I'd help her in the garden."

"Are you thinking the seasickness will be bothering you again?"

I shook my head. "Oh, no, nothing like that."

My grandfather looked at me in an odd way. "All right. I miss my first mate. You're turning into your grandmother's help. You don't want to be working with your old grandfather?"

"Oh, no, it's not that. You know I like working with you." I felt terrible — like I was really letting him down.

"Och, well," My grandfather's wrinkled face eased into a smile. "That will be fine. I don't mind you keeping your grandmother company. It keeps her clear of me, anyway. I'll go and get me tea."

I watched him go. I was beginning to feel more and more useless around the island. I should be helping him. I should be going up the tower. I wanted to be in charge again — to see the ocean lapping the islands, the picture spread out, mountain behind mountain, like the topographic maps we made in school from flour and water, the boats so small they were like toys being pulled along by little boys in a stream.

13

I WAS staring at the tower when I heard Bill Harrison call out, "Hullo, there."

"Hullo." I stood, not knowing whether I should go over and talk to him. He had put down his sketch book and was eating a sandwich.

"Can you tell me something about this lighthouse? How old is it?"

I could see he wanted to talk. I walked closer and stood uneasily in front of him. "Oh, the lighthouse is old. It was built in 1878. But of course they've improved it."

He scratched his beard. "Fascinating. Have you lived here long?"

"Over a year. Well, not quite. I was in Vancouver finishing high school."

"Ah," he took a cookie out of a wet-looking paper bag. "I can't offer you a soggy cookie, can I? No? So, how did you like the city?"

"I didn't like it very much."

"Oh? Here, why don't you draw up a log and sit down." He took out another cookie. He had placed his knapsack on the ground, and I could see what looked like the top of a flask sticking out of one of the open canvas pockets.

I sat uncomfortably on the edge of the log across from him. He was staring at me, and I felt conscious of my bloomer-like shorts, leftover from gymnasium at school. The picture of Morag's neat white fitted shorts flashed into my mind.

If Bill Harrison was drinking now, it didn't show too much, except his words were slurred just a little bit. I hadn't known too many people who drank like that — who carried flasks around with them. The Hebrideans certainly like their drink, but it was mostly reserved for social occasions.

"And why didn't you like the city?"

"I don't know exactly." I looked away, over to the far reaches of the island where the great wind-swept trees were standing in lines. "Maybe because it was noisy and busy and I wasn't used to that at all."

Bill Harrison crumpled up the empty paper bag and put it back in his knapsack. "I don't suppose you were," he said. "And you like this island? Of course, you do." He answered his own question. "It's beautiful. A self-contained world — everything, the ocean, bare rocks, mossy rocks, green for a garden, and even a forest. It's not like the pictures I've seen of lighthouses, which always seem to be stuck out on huge rocks where nothing could grow."

"I know. I think we're lucky. The people in the wave-swept lighthouses — the ones on rocks — they have to live right in the tower. We have our own house. All the keepers would like to get Heron Island — almost as much as the lighthouses right down across from Vancouver."

"All the keepers," he repeated. "Keepers of the light...wave-swept rocks...it sounds romantic."

"It's hard work," I said. "Especially the night watch is hard, and there's no sleeping on the job, that's what the instructions are. My grandfather gets...tired."

"Yes, I expect he would. That was your grandfather in the store, wasn't it?"

I thought that might be a good time to mention my grandfather's health. "He's not feeling so good lately. We're worried about him. He gets out of breath, and gets tired. It's real high in the tower..."

I looked over at the tower as I spoke, at the sheer rise of white wall set against cloudless blue sky. It was very beautiful, but it made me feel shivery just looking at it.

I could see Bill Harrison looking at me again. "And my grandfather," I went on. "There's heart conditions in the family..."

"Then he should see a doctor," he said. "There's a little hospital in Cedar Cove. There are a couple of doctors there."

"He won't go."

"Make him go." It was very clear from his voice that he didn't want to talk about it. I dropped the subject. He was staring at the tower. "There must be quite a view from up there."

"Yes," I said. "You could go up and look if you want. You can see everywhere..."

"Not me. I'd probably fall down the stairs. Don't seem to have the grip on things I once did."

"I don't think I have, either," I said hesitantly. For some reason that made him laugh. I smiled, though it didn't seem too funny to me.

He was staring out at the ocean. "This is some view — some paradise. A person could really *live* here. Compare this to the city. Here, it's carefree and relaxing..." He tilted his head sideways, like he was listening to something.

"Not so carefree when there's a ship in distress or something goes wrong with the foghorn or the *Estevan* can't get in for rough seas..." I stopped. I was beginning to sound like my grandmother.

He looked over at me and grinned. "I suppose you're right. What's a holiday for one is hard work for someone else. Still, it's very beautiful."

I nodded. "I love it here." He fished in his knapsack and brought out a Jersey Milk Bar, melting in the sun.

"Want some?" he said. I shook my head.

He tore open the silver wrapper and scraped up running chocolate with his finger.

"You got any plans," he said, "now that you're finished high school? Are you going to be a lady lighthouse keeper?"

I hesitated. I looked out to the ocean, which lay smooth and unwrinkled like it was joined by two pencil lines. "I don't think so. Not that I can't do the work, and there are women who look after the lights....I'm supposed to be going to Normal School. I've changed my mind, though."

"You don't want to be a teacher?"

I shook my head. "No. And I don't want to go back to the city."

"Well, don't, then." He said it emphatically. He took a pipe out of his knapsack, an ornate pipe with an ivory bowl, filled it with tobacco from a pouch and lit it. His gestures, I noticed, were definite, exact; his fingers long and delicate-looking. He may have been wearing ragged clothes, but he had obviously not lived a difficult life. Beside my grandfather's weathered appearance, Bill Harrison looked soft and cared for.

"I like art," I said. "It was my best subject."

"Oh? Really?" He was looking at me again, a little smile on his face. "So maybe that's the career you have in mind, instead of teaching, is it?"

I was reminded of Mr. Simpson's words about a "career in art." "I'm not sure I'm good enough."

"Well, you never know until you try. Do you have any of your pictures around?" Bill Harrison pulled deeply on his pipe and blew the smoke off to the side. Again, the gesture was a refined one.

"Yes, I do. Would you like to look at them? They're probably not too good."

"I'd like to see them, anyway." He smiled at me, and suddenly, maddeningly, I felt myself blushing.

I was glad that my grandmother was yelling from the porch.

"I've got to go," I said.

"I won't be here long today. Bring me your work tomorrow, Catriona. I'm very interested."

As I walked back to the house I kept thinking of the way he said my name, softly. Then I shook my head. I was acting like a stupid child.

When I reached the house, my grandmother asked me to take the laundry off the line, and I stood for a moment looking at it, watching the breeze move the clothes into odd patterns, the shirts billowing like sails, my grandfather's pants hanging in stiff columns, and I thought again of lines and shapes. And, when I saw Bill Harrison in the distance working again, more than anything I wanted to draw.

14

I HAD a difficult time sorting through my work, trying to choose what to show him. The more I looked, the more I thought how amateurish they were. I finally chose some vases full of flowers, the maple tree in the school yard, the house across the street, and I included the painting I'd done at school from memory, of the island, the lighthouse, the patterning of tall trees against the sky. I knew what I had wanted to put into that picture, but as I looked at it, I could only think of how I'd failed. The colours weren't right. It looked muddy. Like something a child could paint.

My grandmother was grumbling. "Here, Catriona," she said. "Leave off wasting time on that nonsense. There's some sheets need darning, and me half blind, can't work at them like I used to."

"I'll do those later," I said. "I'm taking these pictures to show Bill Harrison."

My grandmother made an "aargh" sound in her throat. "Is he going to be around here every day?"

"I don't know. For a while, I guess."

"Dia, what is the world coming to? Don't you spend too much time with that layabout. And don't you be making too much noise. I could hear the pair of you laughing yesterday. I'm thinking you could hear it on the mainland. And your grandfather was on the night watch and wanting his sleep."

"I'll be quiet." I watched from the window to see when Bill Harrison would finish sketching and start his lunch. When he put down the sketch pad and picked up his knapsack, I gathered up my art work.

My grandmother was staring out the window. "Does the poor man have anything to drink?"

I thought of the flask I'd seen in his knapsack. "I don't think so."

"Well, just you bring him a pot of tea. Here, I'll put the kettle on. He'll need his tea." She ran water into the kettle and put it on the stove. I waited impatiently for it to boil, and then I filled the Brown Betty tea pot.

"Not that," Granny said. "What will he be thinking we are, paupers? I'll get the good tea pot." She brought in the pretty Royal Albert tea set that she only used for company, made the tea in the pot and covered it with a crocheted tea cosy. Then she put everything on a tin tray. I was that impatient for her to finish.

I brought out the tea tray and set it down on a flat stump in front of Bill Harrison. "Look at that. High tea," he said. "You shouldn't have bothered, Catriona."

"My grandmother likes company to have tea."

"That's very nice of her. High tea, *al fresco*," he said. "Like something out of an Impressionist painting."

"I know who the Impressionists were. Mr. Simpson, our art teacher, showed us some of their pictures in a book — Renoir and those people. I don't know what *al fresco* means, though." I poured two cups of tea into the china tea cups and handed one to him.

"Oh, it's just a way of saying out-of-doors."

We drank tea in silence for a moment. "I've got some pictures to show you," I said, hesitantly.

"Good." He had finished his tea quickly and was holding out his cup for a refill. "By the way, are you interested in passing judgement on the sketches I'm doing?" He put down his tea cup and flipped open his sketch book.

"I don't know anything about art, really," I said. "I've never seen real pictures, only the ones in books. Mr. Simpson said you had to look at real pictures to be an artist."

"He's right. But I wish just looking would make you an artist. God knows, I've seen lots of real pictures."

"In Europe and everything?" I stared at him.

He nodded. "In Europe and everything. What do you think?"

There were sketches of trees, of a sailboat anchored in a bay, of barnacled rocks, of seagulls standing on logs, of the lighthouse — the one he was working on now. They were all very exact, almost like everything was measured out.

"I like these," I said. "They're very...clear."

"Clear? What do you mean?" He was peering over my shoulder, holding the tea cup as if it had no handle.

"Well, I really can't talk about art. I guess I mean — real. You know, exact. I like them a lot," I finished up lamely.

"Exact," he repeated the word as if I'd said something nasty.

"Oh, I mean in a good way. I don't know how to describe pictures. That's the trouble."

Bill Harrison took the sketch book from me and closed it. "Yes, you do. You're right. Exactly right — no pun intended. You've spotted it. They are very exact, and mechanical, and uninspired."

"But the pictures look real nice to me. How can you say that? How can you know if they're good?"

"It's like your Mr. Simpson said. By looking at good art. Real art."

"And you can tell good art from bad art?"

"Yes," he said firmly, "I can. Now, run along and bring me the pictures you've done. And thank your grandmother for the tea."

I brought out my work and sat perched on a rock while Bill Harrison went through the drawings, and then turned over the canvas I'd set down back to front. I couldn't tell from his expression what he was thinking.

He seemed to be taking a long time. He had placed the painting against a small rock away from the sun and was standing back from it, looking intently. I wondered briefly if he was trying to think of something to say, so my feelings wouldn't be hurt.

Then he opened the sketch book, turned to the maple tree in the school yard, and then to the vases. Then he abruptly shut the book.

"Well," he said. For an instant I felt like putting my hands over my ears. "Well," he repeated, "he had an eye for talent, your Mr. Simpson. These are good."

I stared at him. "Really? You really think they're good? I don't understand. Your own drawings look so good to me, and you didn't like them."

He nodded. "Oh, they're technically good. I'm a good draughtsman. And you've obviously got a long ways to go. You're right about the perspective. But they're good, Catriona. Take my word for it."

I stared at the open page, the vase full of flowers. "They look so amateurish. I haven't even got the lines right."

He grinned. "Art isn't just getting the lines right. I can get the lines right. There's something else — call it inspiration. Take your painting there."

I looked at the painting, noticing at once the corner where the green — veridien green — had run when it wasn't supposed to. And the sky with its clouds that looked too much to me like the sheep we raised in the old country. Only the tower looked right, sweeping into the sky. I had been thinking of a cathedral when I painted that. Something that made you automatically look up — to a cross, or a bell — or in the case of a lighthouse, to the gleaming lantern sitting under the red top.

"I don't know much about painting. We didn't do too much in school."

"Oh, I can see you've got lots to learn, but you've got something. Something worth cultivating. A natural talent, a natural flair for art. There's real feeling in your painting. Your feeling for the island — I can tell how much you missed it when you were in the city. Now, in my exact drawings, as you put it, there's really no feeling."

"Oh, I'm sure that's not so..." I started to say, but he interrupted.

"Oh, yes, it's true. I keep telling myself I'll get better — too sophisticated, trying too hard. I've been away from it too long. So I tell myself."

I was bursting with curiosity. I wanted to ask him why he'd left off being a doctor, and if he intended to keep on painting. Instead I asked, "Can people make a living painting? A real living?"

"Some do." Bill Harrison was packing up his gear, everything neatly tucked into his knapsack, even the paper lunch bag, tidily folded.

"Are you leaving?" I didn't want him to go. Not yet.

He looked at me and smiled. His smile was warm and curiously intimate. Again I felt myself blushing and hoped he wouldn't notice it. I looked down.

"I'll be back tomorrow. If you want to join the sketching party, I'd like that. Maybe we could sketch the same object, and you can give me hints on what I'm doing wrong."

He smiled again. The smile made him look very young.

I helped him push his small clinker-built boat into the water. "I think I'll row," he said, settling himself in the middle of the boat. "The trouble with motors is you get too lazy." The boat was a pretty one, painted a deep red, the small engine shining silver. Everything looked new. I waved as he rowed off on the bright gleaming ocean. Then I gathered up my work and ran as fast as I could all the way home.

"And what's got into you?" my grandmother said as I rushed through the kitchen.

I paused at the door. "Bill Harrison thinks I've got a talent for art." I said, my voice shaking.

My grandmother turned back to her kneading. "Oh, is that all?"

—15—

WHEN I woke up next morning, the world was full of possibilities. Lying back on the pillow watching the sun drift in slanted lines into the bedroom, I kept remembering what Bill Harrison had said — that I was talented, that my work was good, and warm feelings of happiness and contentment seemed to sweep right through me. In a way, I didn't want to do anything more. I didn't want to shatter how happy I felt.

I got up, threw open the casement window and stared out. The island was bathed in a hazy sun, a heat haze. It was already warm, and everything was perfectly still — no breeze to move the leaves or ripple the grass. I thought how good it would be to sketch again — to capture the hazy look of the day. I took my sketch book and a pencil out of the drawer and went down to help my grandmother with breakfast.

My grandfather had just come in, tossing down his cap on a kitchen chair.

"Dia, Ian, leave that dirty thing outside," my grandmother said as she scooped sizzling bacon slices onto a platter.

"It's not that dirty." My grandfather picked it up and put it on a peg by the door. He threw himself into a chair and looked at the sketch book I'd just put down.

"So you're going to be doing some more drawing?" He sounded out of breath when he talked. "Well, good for you." He took out his red handkerchief and mopped his face. "Och, it's already too damned hot. Dia, I hate hot weather."

I looked at him. "Are you all right?" I asked. "You look a little pale. You know, you ought to get checked up. You really ought to. Even Bill Harrison said that. He said we should make you go..."

"And that's the truth. You should," my grandmother said emphatically.

My grandfather sighed wearily. "I don't want to be hearing anything about it. They only kill you, those doctors. Didn't Duncan McLeod go to the doctor in the old country fine, and then come back sick."

I shook my head. "You know that isn't right."

My grandmother told me to set the table and make sure I warmed the plates first. I put three plates in the warming oven and then turned again to my grandfather.

"Is the work too hard here for you?"

"I've been telling him that," my grandmother said loudly. "We will maybe have to go back to the city. Though God knows there's nothing to do there."

"I'd rather be dead than living in the city. Listening to all that racket, and cars knocking you down in the street. Och, no one is safe there. Listen, the two of you, I'm as healthy as an ox."

My grandmother made the funny sound in her throat. "Aaach, what are you saying? And your own brother dying of a heart attack."

My grandfather poured himself a cup of strong black tea. "That's because he went to live in the city," he said.

After I'd done the breakfast dishes, when my grandmother went out to the chickens, I took my sketch pad and sat in the shade of a cedar tree across from the tower. I had decided to do a new sketch of the tower, with the trees in the background. I was so excited about drawing again. It's odd that I started with the tower. I think it was to assure myself there was nothing scary about it. As if by putting it down I could make it safe.

It looked beautiful in the morning light with the misty heat haze softening it. I decided I wasn't frightened of it anymore, and I would climb it very soon.

I sketched quickly. I wanted to have something to show Bill Harrison when he arrived. I was busy with my sketch when my grandfather came up behind me.

"Catriona," he said, and I jumped.

"Meudal, I didn't mean to scare you." I looked up at him. His face had some colour in it now, and he didn't seem breathless. "I don't suppose you want to come out and do some fishing with me? They're catching big salmon off Nelson Rock."

"I'd like to finish my sketch — "

"All right, don't you worry." He looked out at the ocean. "It's a fine morning for a boat ride, though."

"Are you all right? I worry about you."

My grandfather smiled. "Don't you be worrying about your old grandfather. Even if I was laid up for a bit, which I won't be, there's Colin can take over, and you, once you're up to it. You know how to do everything around here. Och, it's me was worrying about you, Catriona. You were looking very sad when you came home from the city, but now you look better. You're looking happier. It's maybe good for you to be doing your drawings. "

I nodded. "I think it is."

16

I STARTED sketching with Bill Harrison that day. I watched for him, fidgeting impatiently, with my grandmother grumbling in the background. "Don't you be spending too much time with that Bill Harrison. A real doctor and him wasting his time doing drawings. Anyway, if you spend too much time with him, people will talk..."

I looked at her, astonished. "Why?" My grandfather came in just at that moment.

"Why?" my grandmother repeated. "A young girl, a man like that — it doesn't look right, and all."

My grandfather looked at her. "Och, a Dia, why are you making up these nonsense stories? You've been reading too many penny magazines. He's harmless, anyone can tell, likely as not lonely, and wanting someone to talk to."

"He likes being lonely," I said. "He was too busy in the city."

My grandfather looked out the window, his hand over his eyes to shield them from the glare of the sun on the sea.

"There's lonely and there's lonely," he said.

* * *

"What will we sketch? How about that piece of driftwood over there, the big one." Bill Harrison was pointing to a bleached silver-grey carcass that had once been a tree, its branches now rounded and heaved. It reminded me of a huge fossil.

"Sure," I said.

"Then pick your angle, mademoiselle." He swept off his hat in a courtly gesture, and we both walked around the driftwood, studying it.

"I'm sitting here," I said, and settled on a jutting stone to the side, its top softened with moss. I liked the way the wood looked from that angle, almost alive, with gnarled hands reaching out against the sea.

Bill Harrison seated himself in front of the wood, and we both set to work. I was feeling a little self conscious to begin with, aware of his presence, and then I found myself caught up with the lines, trying to put down the way I felt about it, about that object, about how exactly right it was, even when the ocean had finished with it.

But it was hard to put down that rightness.

I was finished before Bill Harrison. I didn't want to bother him, so I walked a little way away and looked at the ocean. I looked from time to time at him, bent over his book, one pencil behind his ear, the other held at an angle, like a dart. My grandfather's words, "likely as not lonely," came into my mind.

I pictured his wife back in the city, someone who looked like the Latin teacher at school, smart and well-dressed, but very stern and demanding, her eyes cold, her mouth disapproving. Someone who probably didn't understand at all why he wanted to paint.

He had finished now, snapped his sketch book shut and stood up. "Well, that's that. So, did you create a masterpiece?"

I walked closer to him, shaking my head. "I don't think so. It's wonderful, though, that driftwood. You know, it looks right where it is..."

"It does. Fine, your turn first. Unveil your drawing, mademoiselle."

I handed him the sketch book, and he whistled. "Whew, what did you see there?"

"It's not very good, is it."

"I didn't say that. It's very imaginative, interesting. Like some kind of monster with arms...that's a funny head you have there, little Catriona." He was smiling when he said it, but I felt terrible, like he was criticizing me.

And I wondered if I did have a funny head — if everything was turning into something terrifying for me.

"It's fine, Catriona, really." He was still looking at my drawing. "Full of sweeping lines, a kind of certainty, that's what I'd call it, like you know what you're doing."

I immediately felt better. "Now." He opened his own sketch book. "If you want to see plodding, here it is." I looked at his sketch, and it was as if we were drawing two different things — entirely different. Bill Harrison's driftwood looked, I thought, a lot more real than mine.

"I think that's good," I said. "It really looks like it. And mine doesn't."

"That's the point." He closed his sketch book and picked mine up again. "You see, you could make this driftwood look exact with a little practice, but you never would."

I frowned. "Why wouldn't I?"

"Because," and he turned and looked at me seriously, and I noticed the intense blue-green of his eyes, "you're too talented to copy."

"Oh," I smiled.

"Could I give you one suggestion, though? You hold your pencil like a murderer clutching a dagger."

"Do I?" I giggled.

"Here, hold it more softly, between the thumb and forefinger like this..." He placed the pencil pointing upwards in my hand, and immediately I was aware of his hand on mine, so I could hardly pay attention. "Now try some strokes."

I made some lines on a page. "That feels good. I was holding it too cramped, I guess."

He smiled at me again, and I felt all tingly.

"Yes," he said.

17

WHEN I remember those weeks, the time I became acquainted with Bill Harrison, they seem a blur to me now. But a blur that is edged with something delicate and golden, like a beautiful frame on a painting. We spent hours together, though my grandmother grumbled constantly, telling me over and over I shouldn't be walking out with a married man.

"What does it matter?" I said to her indignantly one day. "We're only sketching. He knows so much about art. He's like a teacher. Nobody worries if you work with a teacher, whether he's married or not."

"Some teacher," my grandmother had said.

Yet I knew my grandmother was right. He wasn't just a teacher. He made me feel happy and excited and even...pretty.

And all the while I was telling myself that I knew better. That he was married, that it wasn't like me.

There are pictures in my mind of the two of us together sketching, how important I felt when I showed him some of the workings of the island: the foghorn, the generator, the weather station, the small beehive box that housed the thermometer. I remember our foray into the tower, where he whistled at the sight of the spiralling stairs, and neither of us mentioned climbing.

Most of all I remember the day on the other side of the island, the day that made me finally decide to tell my grandparents I wouldn't be a teacher.

It was a place I had come to often the first time I'd lived on the island, but I hadn't visited it since I came home from the city.

"Would you like to see the guano island?" I had run down to meet him as he tied up his boat, and we were now walking along the wharf. That day I remember thinking how he looked neat and clean, the beard trimmed, his pants and shirt pressed. I couldn't help thinking it was all for me. The unkempt, touseled appearance seemed to have vanished. He smelled of some kind of aromatic spice.

"So, Catriona, what's a guano island?" We were near the house now. I could see my grandmother looking out the window. Even from a distance I could make out the expression on her face.

"A place on the other side of this island where the birds nest. They sit in niches. It's very odd looking, very white."

"Good, sounds interesting."

"You have to climb some. Not too much."

"Fine with me. I'm getting in better condition all the time. It's great, this life." He grinned at me, and again I felt the same tingle.

We climbed the bluff and then, holding on to the branches of small arbutus trees and clutching our sketch books, clambered up over mossy rocks, among the soft mint green of the new coverings where tiny purple starflowers and tall white daisies were blooming. The air smelled of wild roses and ocean.

When we reached the top, we both threw ourselves down. The moss was soft and fragrant.

"Whew, that's more of a climb than I thought." He was puffing slightly.

"It's easy the rest of the way."

He took a deep breath. "Look at that. You can see everywhere." I looked. The ocean seemed to vibrate in the sun. The rocks and coves were small crevices, jigsaw pieces.

"It's lovely," I said, and suddenly it came to me, that I was up high but I wasn't the least bit scared.

"You know, this is strange, because...well...since I came back to the island from the city, I've been scared stiff of heights, of lots of things..."

He looked at me. "Well, being scared of heights is quite common."

I shook my head. "This is different. I was never scared before. I loved going to the top of the tower. But now that's what scares me the most. I've tried, but I just panic, really. I freeze, and it's like a..."

"Like a nightmare," he finished it for me.

I nodded.

He had drawn up his knees now and was leaning back, his arms behind him. "It's nothing to worry about — a sudden phobia."

"What's that?"

"A fear that paralyzes you. Lots of people have them. They come and go." He was speaking quietly, and suddenly the fear, out in the open, seemed to be evaporating.

"I'm not getting daft or anything, then?"

Bill Harrison looked at me and laughed. "You're not getting daft. These things happen sometimes, when a person is feeling uncertain, unsure, like you might be now, after the city and your change of plans." He shrugged. "Who knows? And if I could tell you what to do about it, I'd be a millionaire."

"Will it just go?"

"Probably. They say you just go back and keep trying. That's what they say. Easier said than done.

It takes courage. But I know you've got that." He was standing up, brushing off curly bits of moss. "Okay, let's move on, shall we?"

We walked along the top of the bluff. The sun felt wonderful on my bare arms and legs. Behind me the lighthouse buildings were becoming smaller and smaller in the distance, and I felt carefree and happy. It was like getting away — a holiday. I smiled at Bill Harrison, who smiled back. We were walking slowly, side by side, and at that moment I was filled with such happiness that I felt I could break apart.

Suddenly he stopped.

"Whew, look at that," he said, and whistled softly.

In front of us the rocky island had appeared, popping up suddenly, its dark outlines covered with huge white smears, as if somone had emptied enormous paint pots at the top.

And facing us, the seabirds: cormorants and seagulls, all sitting in crevasses, hundreds of them, staring out at us from their white walls. They were like statues in a church. There was an odd silence, as if the birds were half asleep. But they were not. Their eyes were watchful, as they sensed us nearing them.

We clambered down from the bluff. The island was separated from us by a narrow strip of rocks, so that at low tide you could walk across.

But we decided against it, and stood quietly on the shore staring across at the birds.

"What are those black ones?" Bill Harrison was picking up his sketch book. "They're beautiful."

"Cormorants." I said. They were beautiful, the contrast of jet-black against the streaky white, the hooded faces, the shine of the feathers.

Bill Harrison stood up, taking his book with him, and walked quietly to the edge of the shore. There was a slight movement among the birds. He sat down on a huge flattened rock, took off his watch and started to sketch. There was a white band on his arm where the watch had been. I looked at him, noticing the sure movement of the hands, the intensity of his concentration. Then I, too, began to sketch, finishing it quickly, like I always did, and then looked at it. The perspective was all wrong as usual. The birds seemed a bit too big for the rock, but I felt good about the drawing.

And so did Bill Harrison.

"That's nice," he said. We were both sitting, leaning against a log. He was holding my sketch book in front of him. "You've got to do something about all this, Catriona."

"About what?" I said dreamily. The sun was so warm, I felt drowsy. Happy and drowsy.

"Your talent. You've got to study somewhere — Paris, London. You should see real pictures, not reproductions or pictures in books."

"I'd like to see real pictures."

He stretched his arms over his head. "This is the life. Let's run away to the south seas, Catriona. Have you ever heard of Gauguin?"

"I heard of him. But I don't know anything about him."

"Well, he ran away, left everything, didn't care what anybody thought. Left convention behind, got away from the rules and responsibilities."

"Isn't it important to have rules? To have responsibilities?"

"*You* talking about rules — a little Celt like yourself from the romantic islands. Shame on you." He was smiling at me now, and I thought, what a lovely smile, a butterfly smile full of the sun and ocean…

I scarcely remember the journey home. I had no sense of climbing, even of walking. I came home carried on a cloud, floating through the soft air. I walked with him down to the wharf, towards his boat.

"Goodbye, Catriona. When I come back, I'm not sure when — because I have to go to the city — I'll bring some art books and some catalogues."

I stood there and watched him disappearing into the distance, the boat making small frothy wakes that looked to me like strings of diamonds.

18

"WHERE were you?" My grandmother was waiting for me. She was cleaning the copper kettle that stood as an ornament beneath an open kitchen cupboard.

"Just went for a walk on the other side of the island." I started to head for my room.

"Just a minute, young lady. You were out walking with that married man, weren't you?"

"Yes, what of it?"

My grandmother folded her arms. "What are you saying? Och, Catriona, I don't understand you at all now. It's not like you, taking up with a married man."

"I'm not taking up with him." I stood uncomfortably in the doorway.

"Well, I'd like to know what you call it. The man's got a wife, and all."

"He doesn't like her. She doesn't know what sort of person he is..."

My grandmother's hands were on her hips. "Who told you that?"

I shrugged. "I just know."

"And what would that matter, anyway. He's still married. I'm that worried about you, Catriona, that worried. I don't know what your parents would think of you now, God rest their souls."

My grandfather came in just then. "Here," he said, "and what's going on? It looks like a war." He sat down at the table and mopped his forehead with his handkerchief.

"Och, it's this Catriona. I don't know what she's thinking of. She's gone daft, walking over to the other side of the island with that married man."

My grandfather looked at me. "You're not keeping him company, Catriona? You've got too much sense for that, meudal, haven't you?"

"Of course, I'm not keeping him company. We were only sketching. He's only a friend."

"Huh," my grandmother snorted. I said I was going up to my room now, and I left, clapping my hands over my ears to drown out my grandmother's protests.

But I was less bothered by her chatter than by the anxious, tired face of my grandfather as he looked at me, his eyes clouded with worry. And I knew that if they couldn't understand me, I could scarcely understand myself.

Even then, away from him, in my own home, feeling the disapproval of my grandparents, and fighting the guilt that lurked underneath my joy, the remembrance of our time together filled me with warmth and tenderness.

And I felt for the first time part of the world that had been closed to me, of girls who chattered about their dates, girls who walked home with their boyfriends, hand in hand after school, girls who sat with boys in the back rows of the movie house, the boys' arms draped over their shoulders.

And suddenly I wanted to tell someone about Bill Harrison. I opened my bureau drawer and took out some writing paper. I would write to Morag.

"Dear Morag," I began. *"How are you? Have you told your parents yet about your engagement? Let me know. Did you get the job at the sugar refinery?*

The weather has been wonderful and I'm getting a tan, and swimming a lot.

I've got something to tell you, too. This man who comes over to sketch ... someone from Vancouver..."

I stopped. I couldn't get any further. What could I say? How could I explain it? Put down on paper, the facts were exactly like my grandmother was saying. A man older than me, a man who was married. Even if he didn't like his wife, even if he was separated from her, he was married.

I stared at the paper and realized I could not finish the letter. There was no way I could tell Morag about Bill Harrison. No way to describe his gentle voice, his smile, the way I felt protected with him, more sure of myself.

I glanced out the window. The tower was in shadow now as the afternoon lengthened. I determined right there and then to climb it. To dare all, as Bill Harrison had said. Now it would be different. He had given me courage.

I crumpled up the stationery and threw it in the waste basket.

Downstairs, my grandparents were drinking tea. The brandy bottle was on the table, and I wondered if my grandfather was feeling poorly again.

"And where are you off to now, lady?" my grandmother muttered.

"Nowhere."

My grandparents looked at each other. "Have a cup of tea, meudal," my grandfather said. "Let's have peace in the family." He was looking at me pleadingly, and I sat down with them, feeling very uncomfortable, and nibbled at pound cake and drank a cup of tea.

"Well, the summer is going fast," my grandfather grinned at me.

I nodded.

"You'll be looking forward to your year at the Normal School." My grandmother was trying to be pleasant, but the tone was implying that my stay at the Normal School couldn't come fast enough.

"Aye," my grandfather said, "she will."

It was as if I wasn't there at all.

"I'm not going to Normal School," I said. "I've changed my mind."

"What?" My grandmother put down her tea cup with a clatter.

"I'm not going. I don't want to be a teacher."

"Dia, meudal, what are you saying? You always wanted to be a teacher." My grandfather looked puzzled.

Now that I was halfway into it, I charged ahead. "I don't know if I ever really did want to be a teacher. Just when I was small. It seemed the thing to do in the old country, because there wasn't much choice, really. And you wanted me to do it."

"What are you saying?" My grandmother's voice was loud. "Your parents, they wanted you to be a teacher, they were always talking about their clever little girl. Even then you were lining up the little ones some even bigger than you, and trying to teach them. Och, and what would your mother and father think now?" My grandmother's eyes were suddenly full of tears.

"Now, Mairi," my grandfather said softly, "no use bringing up the past. So what do you think you want to do then, Catriona?"

"I don't know."

"Like as not be making beds and cleaning tables, like Morag there. And her a smart girl, twice the head of that Morag." My grandmother blew her nose noisily.

"There's not many jobs for girls now, meudal."

"I know." I looked at my grandfather. "But I shouldn't have to be a teacher if I don't want to."

"I know what it is," my grandmother said harshly. "It's that layabout doctor, turned your head around. You were all settled before. What's he doing? Filling your mind with ideas of doing drawings for a living, no doubt. The likes of him talking to a young girl like you. He wants a good talking to himself. Putting ideas into your head, and hanging about with you, and who knows what will come of it, anyway." Tears were rolling down my grandmother's cheeks.

"He's got nothing to do with it, really. It's my own decision."

"Don't be telling me that. It's that man. I knew from the start. He's the sort that would catch on to a young girl if they got a chance..."

"Don't say that. That's not fair." I stood up and ran outside, my own eyes filling with tears, hurt and anger and guilt all mixed up together. My grandparents had taken something beautiful and made it seem shameful and cheap.

Scarcely knowing where I was going, I found myself in front of the lighthouse. Running as quickly as I could, I crossed the wooden platform and went inside. Quickly I ran towards the stairs, my shoes echoing in the hollow cement. Without stopping, I began the climb up and up the spirals, not stopping to look down.

I didn't know what I was doing, where I was going, but at the back of my mind, I had to prove something. To me, to my grandparents.

On the first landing, I stopped, out of breath, and suddenly where the stairs turned around I could see down below, and a wave of fear hit me so hard that I started to tremble. I stood there, unable to go up or back, like a cat that's climbed a tree and stiffens, frozen on a branch. I felt a terror like I'd never known before. Like I was falling in space, like all the nightmares had come together in this one time. I didn't know how I would get down.

19

SUDDENLY I could hear the door open. It was Colin.

"Colin," I screamed, "help me, get me down."

"What's wrong, Catriona? What happened?"

I held on tight to the railings, my hands wet and clammy. I could hear Colin's footsteps echoing as he ran up the stairs. "Get me down, please. I've hurt my leg."

And then he was beside me, and putting his arm around me, guiding me.

"There now, just you go gentle on that leg. Which one is it? Ah, it's the right one. Easy now, easy." The feel of his arm around me strengthened me, and slowly we came down.

"I've got to sit down." I sat down on the wooden steps outside the lighthouse, legs shaking, shivering all over, cold and sweating at the same time.

"Catriona, are you in bad pain?" Colin was looking anxiously at my leg, and I started to rub it.

"It's getting better."

"But you look terrible. Should we be taking you over to the hospital, then?"

"No, no, it will be all right. I think I must have hit my knee real hard."

"Och, the knee is a terrible sore place to hit."

I nodded miserably. I was calming down now, and feeling ashamed of myself, ashamed that I had to lie about this, ashamed that I had to be rescued from stairs I'd climbed hundreds of times. And disturbed the stove the canning jars were rattling in the huge tub of water, sending thick steam into the kitchen. The weather was still warm, and the kitchen was becoming unbearably hot.

"Seems like it's awfully hot for canning," I said to my grandmother.

She wiped her forehead with the bottom of her apron. "It is. That's the terrible thing about these wood stoves. But you have to be putting things up when they're ready." She glanced at me. "Now, in the city where they have the oil stoves and big ice boxes, then it would be easy. Everything's easier in the city."

"I don't like the city."

"You don't want to be stuck in this sort of place all your life, do you?"

I shrugged. "I don't know."

"Och, you'll have to be making your mind up. And to think..." She stopped herself. "Well, it's a time yet till the end of the summer. Who knows what will happen?"

I didn't answer. I didn't want to get into it again. At that moment, I didn't want to think about anything. I just wanted to drift, making no decisions. Be looked after.

That night, watching the sun setting from my bedroom window, I could smell wild honeysuckle and my grandmother's sweet peas, their trellises outlined in the growing dusk. I wanted everything to remain perfect, like the ocean now, without a mark upon it, no boats, not even a log or a piece of driftwood.

* * *

Morag had left me a movie magazine, and during

the time I waited to see Bill Harrison again, I went through it carefully, admiring the pretty girls with their sleek, clinging dresses, their hair done in waves that cascaded one upon another down their long white necks. I could never look like that, I knew — never be small and perfect — but I took out the polka dot dress Mrs. Johnstone had given me and pressed it carefully. Then I tried to set my hair in waves, tying rags around it when it was wet and drying it in the sun. It was no use. My hair hung in lank strands, looking crumpled, like clothes that had been slept in. I washed it again and left it straight, pinned back with two white barrettes I'd bought in the city, little white bows with pink centres.

20

THE following weekend, after what seemed a lifetime of waiting, Bill Harrison appeared again. I saw his boat, recognized the line of the prow, the distinctive noise of the outboard motor far out in the ocean. I ran upstairs and put on the flowered print dress. I went into my grandparents' bedroom and squirted some of my grandmother's toilet water behind my ears. It was lavender, and smelled like a summer garden. I pinched my cheeks to make them rosy. Then I ran down to meet him at the wharf. I noticed how the blue shirt he wore, with the sleeves rolled up neatly, brought out the blue of his eyes.

"Hello," I said. I felt very shy.

"Hullo, there, Catriona." He was tying the boat up now, and grabbing his knapsack which seemed to be stuffed fuller than usual. "I did bring you some art books and brochures like I promised."

We sat together on a log facing the sea. He looked around and took a deep breath. "Is it ever good to get back. The city is no place for a human being."

"I told my grandparents I wasn't going back, not to be a teacher."

"And how did they take it?" He was reaching into his sack and pulling out two large books.

"They didn't like it."

"Of course."

"But I said it was my decision."

"Good for you. And so it is. I'll tell you, after being in the city, I don't think I'll ever go back.

Let's fly around the world, Catriona. Leave all this." He was smiling at me, and I could feel myself blushing. For the millionth time, I wished I didn't blush so easily.

"All right, now. Here's *A Brief History of Art*." He handed me a large book with a grey linen cover. I spread it open on my knees.

"Not so brief," I said, and he grinned at me.

"And here's another." This one had a blue cover with *The Great Masters* printed on it in gold letters. "And some brochures. The art school in Vancouver — a little out of date I think, but anyhow — and two from New York, one from Paris. I couldn't find one from London."

I spread them out on the log between us, fan-shape, one on top of the other, and I stared at them in disbelief. "New York, Paris, I can't believe it..."

"They do exist, you know." For an instant he looked very young, almost shy.

"But..." I picked up the New York brochure and looked at the cover.

"No buts, Catriona. All positive. Anything is possible. Just remember, courage and determination, that's all."

I put the brochure down. "I'm not very courageous anymore. I tried going up the tower again, and the same thing happened. I froze again. It was terrible."

He shook his head. "The fear won't go just like that. Don't worry about it."

"But on the cliff, that day, I wasn't scared."

"You were with me." He looked at me seriously and I could feel my face growing warm. "You look pretty when you blush, Catriona. It's very beguiling."

I turned away. "Am I embarassing you, then? I won't say another thing. But I'll tell you something that might make you feel better. Turn around and look at me. That's a girl. You see, when I was a surgeon, the last year or so, it was a very bad time for me. I was drinking a little too much, personal problems, I won't go into..." I knew what he meant. "Well, I performed an appendectomy, and I nearly botched it. Thank God another surgeon was assisting. I don't know what might have happened. I was scared, Catriona, really scared. Anyhow, I decided right then and there to quit. Stop being a doctor. Take time out. Do what I wanted to do, get my nerve back."

He looked at me, and I nodded.

"And," he shrugged, "well, to make a long story short, it turned out all right. You see, now I know I wouldn't be scared again, I could do surgery. But, I don't want to. Just like I always knew I could quit drinking, if they left me alone."

I knew who he was talking about. I could picture the stern mouth, the disapproving eyes.

"I'm doing what I always wanted to do, be free. Be an artist, or at least try to be an artist. I knew if I got away, I could test myself as an artist without others trying to run my life for me. Actually, I've got things so under control lately, that I've even popped in at the hospital here. Not to do surgery — too much bother — but they call me when they're extra busy."

"So that's why you've been living out here, painting."

"That's why. And the moral of all this is, well, I don't know what it is. Except that you needn't be afraid. It just takes determination and courage like

I said, to follow your own convictions. And you know, you've been good for me, Catriona. And I'll pay you back, by seeing you develop your real talent..."

"Pay me back. I haven't done anything."

"Oh, haven't you?" His smile was tender now and his blue-green eyes soft in the dazzling light.

We spent an hour or so looking through the brochures, looking at pictures in the art book. He knew so much about paintings. He could talk about Titian, Van Gogh, Renoir, about the paintings he had seen, and their qualities — the thick clumps of paint, the light, and shadow that played over them, the tones, the texture. He knew so much, and he made me want to see them myself, know about them as he did.

"I'd love to see real paintings," I said. "I've never seen any at all."

"You will." His tone was positive.

I wanted that day to go on and on. But it didn't.

"I can't stay too long, Catriona." He stood up and faced me. "I'm working on a painting. I want to finish it off, so I probably won't be over tomorrow."

"Won't you?" I stood beside him, trying to keep my voice from quavering.

He put his arm around my shoulders, gently, barely touching me. I was aware of the mingled smells of aromatic spice and ocean. I started to tremble.

"Just a day, Catriona. I'll be back. You look over the books and think of your great future." He squeezed my shoulder slightly and picked up his knapsack and said goodbye.

After he left, I took the art books into my room, placing them on the bureau side by side, and ran my hands over them as if I were stroking silk.

And that night, hiding from the reproachful glances of my grandmother, the worried frown of my grandfather, I stared out at the great throbbing light that circled, sending its beams into the dark sea. I heard the faint cries of seagulls, growing fainter in the night, and I thought about Bill Harrison and the art schools and the world outside the lighthouse.

21

THE summer was filled with Bill Harrison's voice blending in with the warmth, the dazzling light. It was a time that reminded me of the summers in the old country when Chrissie and I lay on our backs on the hill among the primroses and dreamed of our futures. I learned about the cities Bill Harrison had visited, the treasures he had seen. And always, he would tell me, you'll see these things, Catriona, just you wait. And after you are trained, there will be a first showing. Imagine that, Catriona, your pictures on display in a gallery...

I was too happy, too mesmerized, to ask Bill Harrison where exactly I might study. And now that I look back, it seems to me things were never spelled out.

But at that time I didn't want them to be. I was being handed a wonderful gift, but I wanted only to look at the beautiful wrappings, not look inside.

I also remember my grandmother's admonitions, the tension that filled the house like the continuing and intense summer heat. Until the day I woke up to a sense of something different happening.

"There's going to be a change in the weather," my grandmother said when I came down that morning. "But you probably aren't noticing anything. All you see is that married man you're hanging about with."

"Is there?" I said. I looked out. For the first time in ages, great banks of clouds tinged with grey were floating above the ocean. "It's been too hot..."

"I can't believe it of you, Catriona," my grandmother kept on. "It's not like you. You were always a good girl."

"I'm not doing anything wrong." I stared out at the darkening sea. Waves were coming up.

"Aye, you are. You're keeping company to a married man, that's what. You can't be telling me he's only talking to you about *art*." She said the word with great contempt. "Dia, Catriona, and your grandfather, he's worried, too..."

"You don't need to worry, and I'm old enough to know what I'm doing," I snapped.

I ran up to my room, grabbed my sketch book and rushed out past my grandmother, who was stirring soup furiously.

It was becoming stormy. The sky was darkening, sending alternate streaks of gold, then silver through banked-up clouds. The ocean had turned from light blue to a deep colour — cobalt blue. It was a wonderful day for sketching, trying to put down those colours, that atmosphere.

I took my book out and settled, leaning back against a log, staring at the sea. The ocean was so churned up. I was sure Bill Harrison would not appear that day. I felt disappointed, but I was determined to have new work to show him when he did arrive.

The cloud formations were changing continuously, and again I felt the frustration of wanting to hold something still, to put it down. My finished sketch was disappointing. It was flat somehow, like I was seeing only part of it, not the whole scene.

Like I was seeing it, again, without any perspective.

I tried another sketch, the dock with the huge crane dangling over it, but put it down in disgust. Then another of the dock, then a log, then the square wooden frame of my grandfather's ways. They all seemed wrong. I needed Bill Harrison to look at them. I needed to see them through his eyes.

It was so beautiful, the dark and the light, the clouds now blacker with silver peeking out from under, sending rays like raindrops out of the sky. Like a room with a light on and a door closed, the brightness oozing from the edges.

Then, suddenly, the rain began in earnest. A sudden squall that turned the world into grey mist, swirling the seas, giving them tips of froth. I ran quickly back to the house.

My grandfather was putting on his slickercoat. "Dia, Catriona, what were you doing out in that rain?"

"She's getting daft, that girl." My grandmother was peeling onions, her eyes filled with tears.

"Now, Mairi," my grandfather said.

"You're not going out, are you?" I looked in alarm at my grandfather. "It's terrible, really stormy. Where's Colin?"

"Up trimming the light. He's on the watch. He'll be starting it up. I'm not doing anything hard, meudal, just going to get the foghorn going. It's coming in pretty thick."

"Don't go." I couldn't shake the sudden fear I had. "Or let me go, too."

"Och, you don't need to." He was pulling on his black rubber boots, tucking them into his pants. "No use the two of us getting soaking wet."

"I want to..."

"All right, then." My grandfather looked at me gratefully. It came to me again how little I'd been doing to help.

I put on my long brown raincoat and belted it, tying my scarf around my head, and buttoned up my overshoes. My grandfather and I headed out into the storm. I could feel the wind throwing rain in my face, the drops stinging. I clutched my coat tightly around me. It was a storm like you see in the winter, except that it was not cold.

"I can do the weather," I said.

My grandfather glanced at the wind gauge, now spiralling frantically around and around.

"Aye, you do that..."

The dial on the weather gauge said forty-two m.p.h. and gusting, I was sure, higher at times.

The waves on the sea looked steep. I was used to measuring them by sight. I looked at the cresting water, the long dark ocean ending in peaks of white. Three feet, I thought.

I would phone the weather station.

My grandfather had disappeared into the foghorn building. I didn't want him to get out of sight.

Suddenly I could hear the wail of the siren — the foghorn — and I knew my grandfather had got it going. Not that it was much trouble. The big diesel engine started easily. "Turning on a switch, like driving a car," Colin always said.

I ran to the door of the small building, threw it open and stopped in horror. My grandfather was on the floor, his hands holding his stomach.

"Grandfather," I screamed, "what's wrong?"

He looked at me, his face contorted. "It'll go away. Get me some brandy ..."

"I don't want to leave you."

"I'll be all right. Quick, get me brandy." I ran as fast as I could to the house. My grandmother was stoking up the stove.

"Get some brandy," I screamed. "Grandfather's sick."

"Holy Mother." My grandmother took a small bottle of brandy out of the flour bin, threw on a scarf and coat, and she and I made our way to the blockhouse.

When we arrived, my grandfather was sitting up, the colour returned to his face.

"Are you all right?" my grandmother said. "Here, have some brandy." She handed him the bottle and he uncorked it and took a deep swig and then another one.

"Ah, that's good. Don't fret now. It was nothing, just some bad gas. It's got better. The storm outside took the tuck out of me, that's all."

"No, it was worse than that. You looked terrible," I said. "You've got to see a doctor. You've just got to..."

"Aye, you're going over to that doctor if I have to row myself." My grandmother was standing, her arms crossed, staring at my grandfather.

"All this fuss for a little wind."

"You promise you'll go to the doctor, absolutely promise..."

"If it will make you feel better." My grandfather stood up slowly, holding on to the machinery. "One of these days."

"Soon. Right away."

"All right."

"Here," my grandmother said. "Now you go have the rest. You've got the horn going. And Colin's on the watch..." She reached out and took his arm, and pulled him gently towards the door.

"I can go on my own steam. I'm right as rain."

But I knew he wasn't.

22

THE next morning was warm again, no sign of the storm. I threw on my shorts and sailor blouse, and went down to phone for a doctor's appointment for my grandfather. An unfriendly woman's voice told me he could come over next Friday at one o'clock.

"Not before?" I said. "He's had an attack. That's nearly a week."

"Not before, unless it's an absolute emergency. We're booked solid."

I went out to tell my grandmother, who was in her garden. "Next Friday," I said. "I'll go with him. We'll have to keep an eye on him till then. Where is he now?"

"Out there." She pointed towards the pier, and I could see my grandfather sitting, his legs dangling over the side, smoking his pipe.

"That's good. He looks like he's taking it easy."

I wondered if Bill Harrison were coming over that day. I found myself hitching up my shorts to make them look less baggy. "Do you think I could get some new clothes?" I asked.

My grandmother put down her trowel and looked at me hopefully. "Are you thinking after all of going back to the city to the Normal School? It's in my prayers night and morning. It would make your poor old grandfather happy, Catriona."

I shook my head.

"Well, then, there's no need for new clothes, is there, and we aren't made of money."

"You could make some for me. Maybe I could make some myself. There's some simple patterns now."

My grandmother stood up, hands on her hips. "You, sew? You can't sew." She sounded angry.

"I could learn."

"Och, you were never interested in sewing or even cooking much in the old days. Your head was always in a book. I don't know what's come over you. And, anyways, if you're hanging about with the likes of that hobo doctor, you can go about in rags for all I care." She went back to her digging, scooping up dirt furiously.

I didn't answer. I was looking out at the ocean. Suddenly, I saw something that made me gasp. My grandfather was getting into the *Wanderer*, and I saw what he was after. It was a large log, floating sideways, the kind that might have come off a boom.

"He's not going to try and bring in that log by himself."

My grandmother followed my gaze. "I told him not to be pulling in logs. Colin could do that for him. Dia, what's he thinking of?"

"Where is Colin?"

"In the lighthouse, I think. He said something about going in there."

"I wonder if Grandpa would hear if I called him."

"He's getting to be a long ways off. He'll never hear you." My grandmother looked scared.

"Maybe he will."

I rushed down to the shore, yelling and gesturing frantically. "Come back," I shouted. "Don't get that log." The log was a very large one, with partially peeled strips of bark that made it look from this distance like it was covered with big warts. I knew the struggle involved in bringing home something this heavy.

It was too late. I could hear the steady sound of the *Wanderer's* engine. My grandfather had reached the log. He turned off the engines now to corral it.

"Come back. Don't pull that log," I shouted again, hoping he might hear me with the engine off, but if he did, he was paying no attention. I saw him reach over and hammer a spike into the log, then tie his rope around it and secure it to the cleat. Then he was back at the engine, pulling at the rope again, but there was no response from the engine. And suddenly, as I watched horrified, I saw him grab his stomach and slump over and fall. I could hear his cry, "Oh, Dia," all the way to shore, and then I could no longer see him.

I screamed, "Grandfather," and stood for a moment, frozen. There were no boats on the horizon, nothing nearby. No one to help him. It would take too much time for me to find Colin. I yelled at my grandmother to look for him, and she rushed off in the direction of the tower.

A wind was starting to come up, and I knew the boat would drift. For a moment I stood terrified. I was the only one who could help, and I was scared stiff of rowing out into the middle of the ocean. But I knew I must.

I ran quickly down the pier towards the little rowboat.

23

EVEN now as I try to recall what happened, it is as if the whole thing were a dream. All I knew was that something had happened to my grandfather and it was up to me to help him. I rowed as hard and fast as I could towards the *Wanderer*, conscious of the heat, a heat that somehow seemed thick, so that I was soon covered in sweat. I prayed in Gaelic, "Please let him be all right," and then I drew near the *Wanderer*. As I came alongside, I could see my grandfather sitting on the floor boards, sitting up very stiffly, clutching his stomach, moaning in pain.

I tied the rowboat to the front cleat and clambered on board.

"Grandfather, what's wrong?" I said.

His voice came in gasps. "Catriona, oh, Dia — " Then, abruptly, he leaned over the stern, retched and then vomited. Then, sinking down on the floor of the boat again, he put his hands on his stomach and moaned. His face was contorted. I didn't know what to do for him. I noticed an oilcloth jutting out from under the seat. I pulled it out.

"Grandpa," I said, "I'm going to put this tarp behind your back. Stay calm." I folded up the oilcloth and gently placed it behind his back so that he could rest against the seat. I could see what an effort it was for him to be moved at all. "I'm going to get help. You just rest," I said. His eyes as he looked at me were clouded with pain.

Then I wrapped the cord around the engine and pulled. Nothing happened. I tried again and then again. Listening to my grandfather's moans, I knew I could not waste time. I would have to row.

I unloosed the log from the back cleat, knowing I could never bring in the *Wanderer* with that huge thing attached to it. I thought for a moment. I seemed to be equidistant between the island and Bill Harrison's yellow cottage on the other shore. I would take my grandfather to Bill Harrison. He would know what to do, and the hospital was close. I prayed that he would be home.

I took one last look at my grandfather and said, "I'll help you. You rest." Then I scrambled back into the rowboat and started to row. I hadn't thought that the *Wanderer* could be so heavy — my grandfather called her an eggshell sometimes, she was so tippy in the water — but pulling on the oars I could feel the weight as she moved slowly behind me, ever so slowly. I wished I had a motor in the rowboat — something that would help me to pull the boat faster.

I had done so little rowing during the summer that my arms were rapidly becoming tired. And all these terrible thoughts were running around in my head. What if something happened before I could get the boat to shore? What if my grandfather died? I had to save him. I just had to. Far away in the distance I could see the grey roof of Bill Harrison's cottage. It seemed such a long way away. I prayed again that he was home.

I peered around at the faraway shore hoping that I could see Bill Harrison rush out of his house towards me, but I could see nothing. There was no one around, no ship on the horizon, no boat big or small.

And then I noticed the rowboat becoming harder and harder to row. I was moving sideways, and I realized I was now in the wake of the incoming tide, pushing against me.

My arms were aching, but I pulled with redoubled strength, glancing around from time to time to make sure I was going in the right direction.

The current was flowing strongly now. Small waves and ripples moving steadily towards the shore as the tide came in. Bits of debris, sticks and the bulbous heads of seaweed were floating sideways as the current pulled everything in its wake. My arms were aching so much that I rested for one moment, and as I did, I could feel myself swept sideways with a force that surprised me. I rowed again, frantically this time, feeling as if I were on a treadmill, as if the more I rowed the more I stood still — like I was getting nowhere near the land. For a minute the thought crossed my mind that I would be swept away — that *we* would be swept away, both my grandfather and myself.

Then I told myself that was foolish. I was going to get to shore. I prayed again, little silent prayers. My arms were so sore that I felt as if my whole body was aching, but then suddenly a strange thing happened. I could feel a surge of power in my arms and slowly, slowly, I could see the shore coming nearer. We were inching towards it. It seemed as if it were taking forever, but we were getting closer.

And then I saw something that made me feel like crying with relief. Bill Harrison had seen me. He was running down the beach towards his rowboat, but there was no need. I was close enough to his wharf now, that he was able to run out to the end as I neared it.

He was taking it all in — the *Wanderer* behind me, my grandfather on the floorboards. As I pulled into the dock, I could hear him say, "Oh, my God, Catriona..." Then he was helping me tie up the rowboat and secure the *Wanderer*, and he had jumped into the boat and was bent over my grandfather, saying something I couldn't hear. I crawled onto the dock, and an exhaustion such as I'd never felt before came over me. My arms felt as if I could never raise them again, and in the crooks of the elbows I could see a widening patch of red rash, and on my hands, big puffy blisters.

"Is he all right?" I thought I was shouting to Bill Harrison, but the voice came out in gasps, weakly.

Bill Harrison had his hand on my grandfather's stomach. He pressed gently with his fingers. My grandfather gasped in pain.

"Is this where the pain is?" he was asking.

"Aye." My grandfather's voice was weak. Drops of sweat covered his forehead.

"Was he vomiting?" Bill Harrison asked me. I nodded.

"He's got to get to the hospital right away, Catriona. I'm going to get my neighbour. He's got a car." He clambered out of the *Wanderer*. "You stay with your grandfather," he said and ran down the dock and across the dirt path to the neighbouring cottage.

I pulled myself up and walked slowly to the *Wanderer* and sat down beside my grandfather. "You'll be all right, Grandpa," I said. "Bill Harrison will look after you."

My grandfather turned his head slightly. His face was ashen white as he looked at me, but he had a tiny grin on his face. "Damn quack." He said it so softly I could hardly hear him.

"Don't you move. You'll be all right. You just hold on," I said. It seemed like ages before Bill Harrison appeared with the neighbour, a tall, suntanned man whose shirt was rolled up to reveal huge muscles. He could have been a logger from the size of his arms. And quickly, while Bill Harrison steadied the *Wanderer*, the neighbour, whose name was Steve, jumped into the boat and seemed almost to hand my grandfather up to the dock.

Then Steve clambered out of the boat and, with Bill Harrison helping, scooped up my grandfather in his arms, carrying him easily, as if he were a child, though my grandfather was protesting weakly, "I can walk on me own feet." I walked along beside, noticing how old and frail my grandfather seemed. I had never thought of him like that before. He had always seemed a strong man.

"Will he be all right?" I asked Bill Harrison. My grandfather had closed his eyes and looked like he was losing consciousness. "Do you know what's wrong with him?"

"I hope he'll be all right," he said calmly. "I'd say he's quite hardy, Catriona. I may be wrong, but I think it's peritonitis. Watch it, Steve. There, you sure he's not too heavy?"

Steve shook his head and, just as they were bundling my grandfather into the back seat of Steve's car, a woman came running out of Bill Harrison's cottage. She was small and pretty.

"Bill, what's the matter?" Her voice was full of concern.

"Peritonitis, I think, Margaret." Bill Harrison was making my grandfather comfortable. "Could you get a pillow from the house, quick."

"Of course." She rushed off and quickly reappeared with a thick feather pillow and handed it to Bill Harrison who laid my grandfather's head on it, and stretched him out in the back seat of the car.

"Is it your father?" The woman looked at me. Her eyes were sympathetic and kind.

"My grandfather."

"I'm so sorry, but he's in good hands at the hospital. They've two fine doctors there."

"Yes," I said. And perhaps it was because I was so tired, so worried that it just dawned on me then that this was Bill Harrison's wife. This small and gentle person.

24

I SAT in the front seat of the car as we drove off. I spent the time constantly looking back, alarmed that my grandfather's head seemed to sag, and his breath was rapid and shallow. It seemed like the trip took forever, but it was probably only about twenty minutes.

The hospital was a small building with a steep pitched roof. As we pulled up in front of it, Bill Harrison said, "I'll speak to the doctors. You stay here." And he ran up the front steps two at a time.

Waiting for him to come out with the doctor seemed even longer than the car ride, but eventually he appeared again.

"There's no one around. Just the nurse on duty," he said to Steve. "We'll have to carry him in on a stretcher ourselves."

"Okay by me," Steve said. "No doctors?"

"No. They're both away on emergencies."

"So what are we going to do? You said the old fellow needs an operation right away."

"He does. The nurse said one of the doctors should be in any moment, and we can prep him."

"If they don't come, then what?" I stared at Bill Harrison.

"Let's just hope they come quickly. I'll make him comfortable."

"But, if they don't, you can operate, can't you? I don't want him to die." My words came out in a gasps.

Bill Harrison didn't answer. I couldn't tell if he heard me or not. The nurse had brought out a stretcher, and carefully he and Steve took my grandfather out of the car and into the hospital. My grandfather looked grey and lifeless. His eyes were closed.

"Is he alive?" I was walking alongside the stretcher.

"Yes," Bill Harrison said, "he's alive."

"You can operate if the doctors don't come. Please, don't let him die." I was pleading.

"I'll get him ready. They'll be here, one of them, anyway. The nurse said Dr. Robson was expected back at one, maybe earlier."

"What time is it now?"

"I don't know. Noon, maybe. Here, Steve. Don't rush up these steps. There." He was holding the front of the stretcher, looking back to guide it through the door. The nurse went with them into a back room.

"Can I come?" I shouted as they left.

"No." The nurse's tone was emphatic. And I sat down on the hard seat of a wooden bench and waited.

It was the worst afternoon of my life. No one came out to speak to me, and no doctor appeared. I stared at the bare white walls of the waiting room and listened to the loud tick-tick of a wall clock, and the faraway sounds of voices, voices I could hear, but not understand.

Outside the window the sea was calm and quiet. A heat haze stood on the water, and I was struck with the oddity of two pleasure boats — runabouts — chugging noisily past.

I had never said so many prayers in my life. I prayed for my grandfather to live and get well. My own problems now seemed like nothing compared to this. I kept staring out the window, willing a doctor to appear. The hands on the noisy clock seemed to be standing still. Time didn't seem to be moving on at all.

Maybe, I thought, Bill Harrison had decided to operate after all. If he did, I knew he could pull my grandfather through.

And as I sat there, waiting for what seemed an eternity, I became convinced that was what was happening. Bill Harrison was performing a successful operation. I was so sure of this, that when he appeared I said immediately, "Is he all right? Did it turn out all right?"

"He's comfortable. I wish, though..." He didn't finish the sentence. He was staring out the window.

"You didn't operate?" I stood up and faced him. "Why not? You know how. I don't want him to die. Please." My voice trailed off in a sob.

I could hear him sighing deeply. "No, I didn't. He's ready for the operation, though."

"Ready? He could die. I know he could."

"Now, Catriona, take it easy. Stay calm. I'm sure he'll be operated on very soon."

I stared at him. "Why don't you do it? They'll let you, won't they, the nurse will let you..."

"Yes, they'd let me. But...I can't, that's all."

"You don't want to, that's all," I could hear myself shrieking.

"I want to. Come on, Catriona. I just can't." I stared at him. His face was white. I could see his hands trembling slightly. He was folding and unfolding a piece of paper he'd taken out of his pocket.

"You're scared," I said slowly. "You're scared. And you were telling me about being brave."

I sat down on the bench and started to cry noisily. I could feel his hand on my shoulder. "Now, Catriona, you don't understand..."

"I do." The words came out through the sobs, half strangled. "You'd let him die. You're scared."

"That's not fair."

Suddenly there was the sound of tire wheels on gravel. I looked out the window. A tall, fair-haired man was getting out of the car.

The nurse came bustling out of the back room. "There's Dr. Robson now," she said, and he was in the room and Bill Harrison was talking to him and he was nodding. "I've brought in someone... " Bill Harrison was saying, and they disappeared into the back room, the nurse with them.

Steve was coming out now. He stopped when he saw me.

"Hullo, there. It will be all right. He'll be all right," he said.

"What were you doing? How is he?"

"Keeping him from wandering out. He's delirious. He doesn't know what he's doing. It's all right now, though. We got him down."

"I don't know why Bill Harrison didn't operate. Why didn't he? He should have, he should have." I was saying these words over and over, hardly knowing I was speaking. "If he dies, it'll be his fault." I started to cry again.

"I don't know about that. Can I do anything for you? Are you all right?" Steve was staring at me sympathetically. "Anyone you need to talk to?"

I thought of my grandmother right then, probably worried sick about where we were.

"I think I'll telephone my grandmother. I suppose it's all right. I can phone collect."

"I'm sure it's all right. Listen, I've got to get back. You take it easy, now."

"Thanks," I said.

I could hear my grandmother catch her breath when I told her where I was.

"Oh, Dia, Dia, merciful mother of God," she said, but she didn't go on and on.

I could hear her voice become quiet, patient. My grandmother complained about the little things, but in a crisis, she was always steady. My grandfather's words came back to me. "She's like an old tub at sea, always creaking and complaining. But when she has to get anywhere, she gets there, steady and true." Odd how you remember things like that — funny things in the middle of a crisis.

I told her he was being operated on by Dr. Robson. I was sure he was in good hands.

"I'll say my prayers," she said, and I told her I would get back to her as soon as I knew anything.

25

IT seemed like days, but probably it was more like two hours when Dr. Robson came down the hall to talk to me.

He was in a white hospital coat, and I thought I could see traces of blood on the front of it.

I stood up. "How is he?"

"You're...the daughter?"

"Granddaughter."

Dr. Robson nodded. "Ah. Well, he'll be okay. Not out of danger, but I think we got it in time."

"Oh, thank God, thank God." Tears filled my eyes.

"He's a pretty strong fellow, but he hasn't been looking after himself too well. Peritonitis is just a symptom. He hasn't been looking after his stomach and his heart doesn't sound too good. He's going to need rest. Lots of it. But he'll make it, if he's careful."

Relief flooded over me, making me feel almost weak.

"Can I see him now?"

The doctor shook his head. "He's asleep. Tomorrow would be better. He'll be here for a while yet, so you'll get a chance to see him. I understand he's a lighthouse keeper."

I nodded.

"Well, he won't be clambering around on that island for a good long while."

"No," I said.

The doctor was looking at me, a small smile on his lips. "Dr. Harrison tells me you pulled him over here — rowed across, pulling a big heavy boat."

I nodded.

"You probably saved his life, you know. You were very brave."

I bit my lips to keep the tears back. "Thank you. Where is...Dr. Harrison?"

"Oh, he went home a long time ago. Didn't you see him? I didn't really need him."

"Went home?" I stared at him.

"And you, young lady, are you all right to go home? Do you want to telephone anyone?"

"I can get home," I said. "I'll telephone my grandmother first."

"Now, God be thanked," she said when I told her. She was having trouble controlling her voice. "Can we be visiting him, then, Catriona?"

"We'll have to arrange about that. But I'm coming home now."

"You be careful then, Catriona. What would I do without you? Can you get back all right?"

I said I would, and her voice trailed away.

I made my way to the *Wanderer*. Now that there was not the panic I had felt trying to start the engine last time, I pulled on it over and over, calmly, until finally it went with a sputtering explosion. And quickly I was chugging along the passageway, pulling the small rowboat behind.

I glanced back at the bright-yellow cottage, Bill Harrison's house, and pictured the sympathetic look his wife had given me. I felt angry in a way I had never felt before. Angry at him and at myself.

The sticky oppressive heat was beating on me. I wished I had a hat. The heat was making me giddy.

I took a handful of water and threw it on my face and over my head.

And what I was picturing was Bill Harrison standing there, trembling, his eyes full of fear, willing to let my grandfather die because he was afraid.

And my grandmother's words rang in my mind. "Talk is cheap, Catriona." I pulled the tiller gently towards me and made for shore.

It had been all talk. The incandescent heat haze shimmered on the horizon, and I thought he was like that — like something that looked beautiful, substantial, but vanished when you reached its centre.

And I knew instinctively that at the centre I was not like that.

I also knew, but only in a dim way, at that point, that someday I would be able to see Bill Harrison more objectively, and to understand the part my own imagination had played in our friendship. And someday I might be able to acknowledge the door he had opened for me. One I would have to walk through by myself.

I tied the boat up to the wharf and ran up to the house. My grandmother was waiting for me at the pier, and I told her in detail what had happened, watching her hold back the tears that welled up in her eyes.

"I thank God." She said it quietly, her hands perfectly still in her lap. "You were a brave girl, Catriona. You saved his life, like as not."

"I'm glad I was around. He's going to be all right," I said. "I know he will. But he's got to take it easy."

"Easier said than done. He's stubborn, that man."

"I know, but I'll help, I'll be here..."

"You're not going anywhere, then?"

I shook my head. "No, I can help. I know I can. I've done the work before. Colin and I can do it till he's well." We talked quietly for a while, drank a cup of tea, and then I said I wanted to go out for a moment.

"You should rest, Catriona. You must be worn out."

"I had a rest coming over. It's all right..."

"Don't you be long, Catriona," my grandmother said. "Don't let anything happen to you."

"I won't." I had never felt so secure in a decision. I was needed now. It was my responsibility. I wasn't sure what the future held, but one thing I knew. If I was to have an art career — whatever I did — it would be initiated by me.

I was nearing the lighthouse now, and quickly I walked up the wooden steps, across the ramp and through the arched door.

Without looking, I started up the steps, higher and higher as they spiralled and turned. For one brief moment my legs felt shaky and weak — but then, I told myself, why wouldn't they be after all I had gone through. I kept on, one foot after the next, up and up, excited, a little frightened, until I was finally there, at the top — there in the room with the great prismatic light, glittering and shining in the sunlight. I paused for a moment, and then walked over to the rail and peered out through the glass.

I could see everywhere. The sea was like a large snake, iridescent in the light. There were humped mountains covered with small trees, and beyond a lake and beyond that more mountains.

And I was seeing it all in its dimensions. My world was no longer flat. I was beginning to put it all into perspective.

A une charmante
CHOCOLAT
de Brisy